Ivy & Intrigue:

A Very Selwick Christmas

A Novella

by

Lauren Willig

Author of *The Secret History of the Pink Carnation*

For all my readers,
with love
and thanks.

PROLOGUE

Sussex, 2003

The Uppington Hall visitor website had claimed the house was walkable from the train station.

But, then, websites claimed a lot of things. As I had sternly lectured the undergrads in my Western Civ section the year before, you can't trust everything you read on the internet. Excellent advice, if only I had listened to myself before getting on a train to Kent in subzero weather, armed with nothing but my mobile, a book to read on the train, and a Cadbury fruit and nut bar.

I turned up the collar of my pea coat, wishing I had worn something more substantial. A fine dusting of snow had fallen the night before, crisping nicely into ice overnight. It looked very pretty on the ground. It felt very slippery under my high-heeled loafers. From what I had seen so far, the concept of shoveling was not one widely known in the old country. I had the direst forebodings as to what this portended for my flight back to New York the next day. Snow and Heathrow don't exactly go together like peanut butter and jelly.

I had one day left before I flew back to New York for Christmas, one day to kill before I descended back to the bosom of my family for presents, gingerbread and familial sniping. I suppose I could have gone to the archives—they were still open—but I was already on vacation in my head, even if the archives weren't. Colin and I had held our own private Christmas celebrations the night before, quaffing spiked cocoa and exchanging presents in my tiny basement flat, under the benign auspices of a miniature potted fir tree I had picked up for ten pounds at the local Marks & Sparks.

It was a farewell party as well as a Christmas one, the last time we would see each other until 2004. Colin had something going on in Sussex that night. And I? Theoretically I was meant to be packing, but since all I was bringing home was a satchel full of bulky and badly wrapped Christmas presents and my computer, that had taken me all of half an hour. In short, I was restless. Restless and bored and feeling just a little sorry for myself at the prospect of a lonely evening with no one to talk to but Oliver, the mini-tree. I needed a diversion, and I had the very one in mind.

I was going to take a day trip to Uppington Hall, historic seat of the Marquesses of Uppington.

As I had noticed over the course of my researches, the Uppingtons tended not to be terribly creative with their choices in nomenclature. The

London mansion, which had survived the Blitz but succumbed to financial crisis, had been called Uppington House; the country estate, Uppington Hall. No surprise that a nineteenth century daughter of the house, Lady Henrietta Selwick, had named her stuffed bunny Bunny. Anything else would probably have seemed uncomfortably revolutionary.

The house had stayed in the hands of the Marquesses of Uppington, but like so many others they had found it necessary to open it to the public, using the proceeds to do useful things like keep the roof in repair and halt the steady flow of paintings and objets d'art to the Sotheby's showroom. They couldn't make that much money off it; as historic houses go, this one was not as well known as Blenheim or Chatsworth, and it was a bit too far off the beaten track for the casual tourist trade.

Just how far off the beaten track, I was in the process of finding out.

I had taken the train to Upton Station on the commuter line that ran down past Maidstone. Upton, in case you haven't guessed it, was a corruption of Uppington. At least, that's what the website claimed.

I wasn't sure how much faith I had in that website anymore. Shoving my gloved hands deeper into my pockets, I hunched my shoulders against the cold, sinking my chin into the folds of my scarf all the way up to my nose. I had been walking for a good fifteen minutes now and I still hadn't seen any sign of anything that remotely resembled a massive marble mansion.

A signpost at the station had read "To Uppington Hall". The fact that it had been hand-lettered ought to have filled me in that this was not exactly one of your more professional operations. Instead of a sidewalk, the pointy end of the sign indicated a path. Someone had graveled it at some point, but most of the gravel had worn off, leaving a twisty trail of frosted mud between winter bare hedgerows. The sign hadn't bothered to indicate just how far it actually was to Uppington Hall. Halfway to the next county? Somewhere over the rainbow? Hadn't they heard of such things as shuttle buses?

A taxi, a taxi, my kingdom for a taxi.

Just as my toes decided to part company with the rest of my feet, I spotted it, the rounded top of a dome poking over the trees like a hiccup in the winter gray landscape. There were lights burning in the windows, glorious yellow lights with their implication of inhabitation and warmth. If the house had been closed, I don't know what I would have done. Cried, perhaps. Candles, electric ones from the look of it, had been placed in all the lower story windows. There were evergreen wreaths decked with red bows hanging from the twin gateposts that guarded the drive. The gateposts looked too new and too close to the house to be original; my guess was that they were a twentieth century addition. The nineteenth century drive had undoubtedly been much longer, with a proper gatehouse to guard the entrance. I wouldn't be surprised if the gatehouse was now someone's country house, sold off with most of the surrounding property as death duties had taken their toll in the 1920s and 30s.

But it was pretty and festive and I felt relief seep up to warm my cheeks as I trudged up to the front door, shaking icy bits off my shoes and trying to stamp the feeling back into my feet.

Before I could reach for the handle, a uniformed footman in livery and periwig swept open the door, and I wondered, for one bewildered moment, whether I really had stumbled back in time, into a Christmas long ago. Maybe those candles weren't electric after all. The air smelled delightfully of mince and cinnamon and evergreen branches. Young ladies with their hair in bunches of curls on either side leaned together to gossip behind their fans while white-wigged footmen stood impassive at each entryway, looking neither left nor right.

That's when I spotted the reception desk.

Reality snapped back into place. Beside the desk, a large easel read "Uppington Hall Regency Christmas, 15-23 December", with a clumsily drawn picture of the house beneath it. Superimposed over the house, in much smaller print, the poster went on to list the various activities available: costumed re-enactors, a traditional caroling session, Christmas pudding stirring in the old kitchens, a dress-up selection for the under-twelves.

Now that I knew to look for them, I could see other visitors roaming about, looking as out of place as I did in their jeans and sneakers, making faces at the costumed actors and elbowing one another as they leaned over the exhibit cases. I shouldn't have felt disappointed, but I did. I knew the house was open to the public now. I wouldn't be there if it weren't. But it was still a weird sort of letdown to see other public there, too.

I wandered inside, feeling a bit off-balance, my ears still ringing from the cold and my head swimming from the bizarre juxtaposition of past and present. Then, of course, there was the house itself, although to call it a house did it less than justice. It was to other houses what Cartier was to Kay's. If I had found Selwick Hall impressive, Uppington Hall was in another league entirely. It made Selwick Hall look like what it was; a relatively modest gentleman's residence, the sort of place that could be comfortably passed on to a younger son.

The entry hall soared up three stories to a great dome decorated with pictures that were so high up that they appeared as little more than a brightly colored blur. Two branches of a splendid, curved staircase swept up from either side of the hall to meet at the second story, the landing forming a circle around the entire circumference of the dome. Longer hallways branched off to myriad wings, which stuck out from the center like the spokes of a wheel. The staff had closed off the base of the stairs, looping greenery from one post to the other. It was festive, but it was still a barrier.

I wondered if the family still lived in those upstairs rooms. I wondered if they looked like Colin.

That was silly. Of course, they wouldn't. This side of the family was descended from the direct male line, through Lord Richard's parents to his older brother, Charles, to Charles' oldest son Peregrine, and so on down the line, all of which was a very long way of getting around to the fact that Colin's branch had split off a full two hundred years before, with the marriage of Lord Richard Selwick to Miss Amy

Balcourt. It was their line, intermarried at some much later point with that of Lord Richard's best friend, Miles Dorrington, that had inherited Selwick Hall and begat a son who begat a son who begat and begat until someone finally begat Colin.

As you can tell, I really hadn't paid much attention to the more recent bits of Colin's family tree.

What it all came down to was that Colin's relationship with these Selwicks, the current Marquess of Uppington and his family, was so tenuous as to be practically nonexistent. Even so, I still felt a bit like Elizabeth taking a tour of Pemberly behind Darcy's back.

That was the problem of spending too much time in the early nineteenth century. There were times, I admitted to myself, loosening the buttons on my coat as the warmth of the house began to seep through the fabric, when I did fall into the trap of conflating Colin with his notorious ancestors, linking him in my head with the activities and surroundings of people who had died well over a century before.

Was that why I hadn't wanted Colin here with me? Because I didn't want to see him as out of place as I was in the house that, in my head, was still partly his home?

Grimacing to myself, I fumbled in my bag for the three pounds for my ticket price, my chilled fingers clumsy among the coins. If anything should kill off that fantasy, it should be the having to pay for admission. I doubt the Uppingtons had charged Amy when she arrived there for her first Christmas celebration.

Nor would she have been wearing her coat inside, like any other museum-goer. Dating an off-shoot of an off-shoot of an off-shoot did not make me a member of the Uppington clan, at home in their hallowed halls. I might be immersed in their family papers, but, when it came down to it, I was just another American tourist with a red nose from walking from the train station and shoes that spread slush across the crackling brown paper that had been spread out to protect the old marble floors.

It was a good thing I was going home to New York for Christmas. I needed a dose of reality, something to bring me back down to earth. Dating a descendant of the Purple Gentian was wonderful in a vast number of ways, not least of which was the man himself, but it didn't do much to help me sort out that tricky line between daydream and reality.

Surrendering my three pounds, I was handed in return a cheaply printed pamphlet, with a rough sketch of the floor plan on one side and hours for the museum and gift shop on the other. "There are no guided tours today," the friendly woman at the desk informed me, her ponytail bobbing as she rammed shut the register drawer. "But the re-enactors are there to answer your questions."

Huh. I had thought they were there to lend a period feel. Apparently, they were multi-purpose items.

"You can go to any of the rooms marked as open on the map," she continued. "The blocked off areas are still used by the family."

Thanking her, I glanced down at my map as I wandered away to make room for the next person in line, a harried looking woman with two small children, one of whom could be heard plaintively wailing, "Why do we have to go *here*? Those people look funny!" The larger part of the map was blocked off. The only bits open to the public appeared to be the main reception rooms on the lower floor and a series of smaller rooms that branched off them. And the gift shop, of course. There was always a gift shop.

Too bad I had already given Colin his Christmas present. I could have gotten him an Uppington Hall tea towel and really freaked him out.

Probably for the best that I had played it safe and given him a scarf instead. By coincidence, he had gotten me one, too. We were still in that phase of the relationship where generic gifts were safest. We would have the warmest necks of any couple in London. It could have been worse; it could have been slippers. Or soap on a rope.

Grand double doors had been propped open on one side, revealing a reception room vast enough to double as a high school gym. The carolers were congregating there, clustered in one corner, their music stands very small and spindly against the massive proportions of the room itself, with its high ceiling, intricate plasterwork, and glittering display of Venetian mirrors. Long settees lined the walls, interspersed with busts of dead monarchs and marquesses resting on chunky columns of matching marble.

Matching fireplaces on opposite sides of the room were topped, not by mirrors, but by an imposing pair of portraits, far larger than life, of a couple in formal dress. The lady wore a towering confection of egret plumes in her high-piled hair and enough emeralds to keep a small Latin American country in business for some time. The artist had painted her eyes the same vivid green as the gems at neck, ears and wrist. There was a mischievous quirk to her lips, as though she had just spotted a joke that everyone else had missed. The man on top of the opposite side of the room had an amused air about him, too, but in a calmer way. His lips were still, but his eyes were smiling. It didn't take peering at the brass plates at the bottom of the paintings to guess who they must have been: my very own Lord and Lady Uppington, presiding over Uppington Hall in paint as they once had in the flesh.

One could almost picture them stepping out of their frames to play host, sweeping aside the tourists and signaling the silent harp into song.

The re-enactors were all wrong; from their costumes, they were late Regency, 1820 or so, rather than the pre-Regency period in which I was interested. There was a wide gap between the two, in style and in outlook. But the servants would probably have looked very much the same, in their livery in the Uppington colors, and so would the pre-Victorian Christmas decorations. If I ignored the "party guests" and the other tourists, it was just possible to picture what it might have been like two hundred years ago, when Lord and Lady Uppington had held Christmas at the family seat.

I paused, struck by the symmetry of it. It would have been almost exactly two hundred years ago, wouldn't it? December 1803 to December 2003.

It would have been Colin's ancestors' first Christmas together after the mad upheaval of their marriage the previous spring. There would have been candles, just as there were now, and the smell of oranges and cloves.

There would have been gaily gowned ladies and excited children and tables laden with ratafia biscuits and dried fruit and the inevitable sticky sweet slices of mince pie....

CHAPTER ONE

Deck the hall with boughs of holly,
Fa la la la la la la la la.
'Tis the season to be jolly,
Fa la la la la la la la la.
           -- "Deck the Hall"

Sussex, 1803

"Darling, you've already had three," said Amy, scooping her new nephew away from the buffet table before he could hook another mince pie in his grubby little fingers. His fingers were grubby with mince, but that was beside the point.

"Four!" said Peregrine proudly. He had just learned to count and he was justifiably pleased with the new skill.

He looked expectantly at Amy. His display of his new party trick already had a proven record of garnering tangible rewards from impressionable adults. Aunty Amy was no exception.

"All right," Amy capitulated. She scooped up the slice of pie and offered it down to him. "'Tis the season, after all."

"Mmmph," agreed Peregrine, mashing a large quantity of mince against his face and a very little bit of it in his mouth. At least that way, thought Amy optimistically, he wasn't likely to get a stomachache, even if his velvet suit wasn't likely to survive until Christmas Day.

All around her, Uppington Hall was decked for Christmas. Greenery dripped from balustrades and portrait rails, from moldings and doorframes. Irreverent crowns of prickly holly perched on the heads of marble busts of past monarchs, visual symbol of the Uppingtons' favor at court over the generations. Only the painted deities on the ceiling had been spared decoration, and that, Amy, was sure, was only because her mother-in-law couldn't reach them. Even the blackamoor candelabra positioned on either side of the door bore belts of red ribbon around their waists.

It was Amy's first Christmas as Uppington Hall, principal seat of the Marquesses of Uppington, her first Christmas as part of the Uppington clan, her first Christmas as a married woman. In grand seigneurial fashion, the Uppingtons were holding open house for Christmas Eve, with all of the local gentry invited to partake of mince pie, Christmas pudding, and a variety of less seasonal delicacies. The air smelled delightfully of cloves and orange peel and the boys of the local church choir were singing away in the corner of the room, their pure, high treble voices lifted to the heavens in a song of praise.

A gloved finger tapped her on the shoulder. "The season for what?"

"Jane!" Amy launched herself at her cousin.

Fortunately, Jane was accustomed to Amy's ways. She braced herself in preparation for just such a move and so was spared careening into a bust of the first Marquess of Uppington. The Marquis had suffered indignities enough for one holiday season. His flowing marble locks were adorned with a chaplet of holly from which the berries were already beginning to fall. Amy's mother-in-law believed in leaving no unmoving surface undecorated.

Amy had her suspicions about the moving ones as well, but since she seldom stayed still, she figured she was safe.

Now, she gave an extra little bounce as she gave her favorite cousin an exuberant hug. "When did you get here? I didn't hear you arrive."

Jane smiled the enigmatic smile she appeared to have perfected during her time abroad. "You weren't meant to."

Amy rolled her eyes. "You can't claim to be here incognito. Not with the whole family in tow."

Uncle Bertrand and Aunt Prudence had arrived the night before, in an antiquated carriage laden with assorted offspring, Aunt Prudence's embroidery bag, and one agitated sheep. The sheep, apparently, was a Christmas present. Amy only hoped it wasn't intended for her. She had had enough of her sheep in her upbringing in Shropshire, when the French

Revolution had exiled her to the care of her aunt and uncle.

It had been Amy's mother-in-law's idea to invite Amy's family to join them all for Christmas at Uppington Hall, the official seat of the Marquesses of Uppington. It was, Amy had to admit, a very thoughtful notion. She was more pleased than she cared to admit to have familiar faces around her.

Well, maybe not all the familiar faces. A sharp object did its best to make a dent in Amy's left side. It turned out, upon inspection, to be a fan.

Only one woman carried a fan that pointy and wielded it with such deadly precision.

"Incognit*a*," snapped Amy's former chaperone, Miss Gwendolyn Meadows, driving the point home with another jab of her fan. "Incognita, not incognito. Despite a masculine occupation, one need not abandon the feminine persona."

Jane's lips turned up at a private joke. "Except, perhaps, when it might be expedient so to do?" she suggested demurely.

Miss Gwen sniffed. "Expedient," she allowed, "but *never* ungrammatical."

There had been an untold story in that sniff. Perhaps more than one.

Amy looked quizzically from Jane to Miss Gwen, trying not to look as left out as she felt.

Only eight months ago—not that she was counting—they had been a team, the three of them. She was the one who had started it all, after all. It had been her idea to track down the Purple Gentian, her idea to join the ranks of those cunning men who slipped from shadow to shadow, outwitting Bonaparte at every turn. But she hadn't managed to stay quite shadowy enough, and in the space of one fatal evening, everything had changed. Now it was Jane staying with her brother in her old house, Jane outwitting Bonaparte, Jane getting written up in the illustrated papers as the most daring thing to enter the scene since espionage went botanical.

Amy knew she shouldn't resent Jane for carrying on with their plans. The point was the goal, not the individual agent.

But she did resent it. It wasn't logical, and she didn't like it, but there it was. *She* wanted to be the one making daring midnight raids on the Tuileries Palace and composing insulting little notes to leave on Bonaparte's pillow. She had spent years plotting and scheming to find the Purple Gentian and join his League. It was ridiculous beyond all things that the very accomplishment of that goal should have been the cause of both of them being barred from Paris and espionage altogether. It was like of the Greek tragedies her father had loved so well, where the accomplishment of a wish led to its own destruction.

Not that Amy was complaining, she told herself hastily. If she had to choose between her husband and another season's spying in France... well, Richard was solid and real and kept the bed warm on cold nights and never once thought it was odd or unladylike when she wanted to practice shooting at targets or climbing over fences or other skills that might just come in handy again. There were many spies in the world but only one man she could imagine spending the rest of her life with.

They were happy, really they were. And no one could say they hadn't made good use of their exile. Together, they had cobbled together a comprehensive curriculum for the training of secret agents, combining Richard's experience in the field with some of Amy's more inventive ideas to produce a program that purported to plan for every possible contingency. They were still working out some of the kinks in the curriculum, but their first batch of pupils were coming along quite nicely.

But teaching wasn't the same as doing. If she minded it, how much more must Richard?

She had caught him, more than once, plotting out routes on the atlas that he would never again follow, and, when he didn't know she was looking, she had seen him staring broodingly at his old cloak and mask, tokens of the work that was lost to him.

No matter. It was Christmas; they were together; and they were *happy*. 'Twas the season. It was practically mandatory to be happy at Christmas. She was happy. She was, she was, she was.

Even if she was just a teeny tiny bit jealous of Jane.

"How long are you back for?" Amy asked her cousin.

"Just past Christmas," said Jane. "I don't like to leave our affairs unattended for that long."

"I'm glad you were able to get back at all," said Amy, trying to sound enthusiastic.

Jane smiled down at her. "You made it very easy for me. How clever of you to find relatives with an estate so near the coast."

Despite herself, Amy grinned back. She knew better than to ask Jane exactly how Jane had made her way from Paris or how she intended to return. Jane kept her own counsel on such matters. It was a trait Amy had found maddening while they were working together. One could never tell quite what Jane was planning until she had done it.

Discretion was something Jane had always done very well. She, on the other hand....

It was her indiscretion that had bollixed Richard's career as the Purple Gentian.

"Well, happy Christmas!" she said, so forcefully that Jane blinked and Miss Gwen frowned. But, then, Miss Gwen always frowned. It was when Miss Gwen smiled that one had to worry.

"Hmph," said Miss Gwen. "Christmas hasn't happened yet. We have no idea if it will be happy or not."

"Spreading good cheer as always, I see?" Richard strolled over to join them, accompanied by two women.

One of the ladies was roughly his own age, with pale blonde hair clustered in curls around a china oval of a face. The other, her mother by the look of it, had the determined look of the faded beauty, trying to make up in too-rich fabric and jewels what she could no longer accomplish with her face. Her white hair had been swept into an elaborate coiffure topped with a diamond parure. A very silly thing, Amy thought, to be wearing to a county affair, even one at the home of a marchioness. The older woman clung very determinedly to Richard's arm.

Detaching her without visible sign of effort, Richard moved in a touching show of husbandly devotion to his accustomed place by Amy's side.

It was, thought Amy, rather clever of him. It put her in between him and Miss Gwen's fan. He was no fool, her husband. He smelled rather nice, too. Like citrus. With a hint of cloves. He must have been raiding the gingerbread again.

Quick to deflect any accusations of good cheer, Miss Gwen favored Richard with her steeliest stare. "Don't expect me to start spreading goodwill towards men. Useless, the most of them."

"What about peace on earth, then?" inquired Richard blandly.

"Bah," said Miss Gwen.

"Bah?" inquired the older of the women Richard had brought with him, in tones of frigid disbelief. *"Bah?"*

Miss Gwen looked down her nose. "One bah was entirely sufficient. There is no need to imitate a herd of sheep."

"Sheep?" Uncle Bertrand might be slightly deaf when it came to social niceties, but any mention of his favorite subject brought him bounding to his feet. He crossed the room in record time. "Did I hear sheep?"

"Ah," murmured Richard. "The pitter-patter of playful sheep."

"I had a lamb once," said the blonde woman helpfully. "But it was a very long time ago."

"Never too late for another," said Uncle Bertrand heartily, clearly empathizing with her plight.

Amy hastily intervened. "I don't believe we've been introduced," she said, forestalling Uncle Bertrand before he could inquire after the name, age, and cause of death of the late, lamented little lamb.

"Forgive me for neglecting my duties," said Richard. "Allow me to present Mrs. Ramsby and her daughter, Lady Jerard." He carried on with the introductions, presenting Miss Gwen, Jane, and Uncle Bertrand in turn, but Amy heard nothing after that second name.

Baroness Jerard. Here. Now. For Christmas.

Why hadn't anyone warned her?

Amy must have said the civil thing. She must have bowed or curtsied. Early training did win through, even when one's mind was entirely elsewhere.

No one had told her that Lady Uppington had invited Richard's.... Oh, heavens, Amy didn't even know what to call the dratted woman. First love? First disappointment? Careless betrayer of valiant English agents?

There wasn't an exactly a one word tag for the-woman-who-broke-his-heart-and-caused-the-death-of-his-second-closest-friend.

At times, the English language was sadly lacking in crucial terms.

CHAPTER TWO

Now bring us some figgy pudding,
Now bring us some figgy pudding,
Now bring us some figgy pudding,
And bring it right here.
-- "We Wish You a Merry
Christmas"

Amy pasted a smile onto her face and took inventory of her—well, not rival. She couldn't call the other woman a rival when they weren't in competition. They had better not be in competition. Her predecessor, then, even though there was nothing deceased about her.

Lady Jerard—Deirdre, as Richard had called her—was everything Amy had imagined and dreaded. Hair like silk floss, lips of rose, teeth of pearl, blah, blah, and so on. She could see how Richard had once composed reams of poetry to this woman; the material practically wrote itself. The violet of half-mourning perfectly set off Lady Jerard's roses and cream complexion. Amy felt suddenly very conscious of the whopping case of wind burn she had acquired earlier that afternoon on a last minute mistletoe expedition, Lady Uppington having deemed the quantity already acquired woefully insufficient.

Amy's cheeks pinkened with more than windburn at the memory of the use to which that mistletoe had already been put. The thought cheered her up immensely, and she slid her gloved hand into her husband's.

Squeezing her hand, Richard smiled down at her, his own peculiar, familiar smile, the one that he kept just for her. Amy felt the fog that had begun to descend on her lift. The candles sparkled like stars off the long, Venetian mirrors set into the walls, and, in the background, the choir was singing again, like angels calling from the mountaintops. Everything was cinnamon-scented and perfect and just as it ought to be.

Until a shrill voice intruded. "So you're the wife, are you?" said Mrs. Ramsby.

Amy could see Miss Gwen stiffen with offense at Mrs. Ramsby's tone. It wasn't that Miss Gwen minded on Amy's behalf; she just disliked rudeness in others. It took the edge off her own.

Amy smiled cheerfully at the faded beauty, baring as many teeth as possible. "As far as I know." She batted her eyelashes at Richard. "You do have only the one, haven't you, darling?"

"Minx," said Richard fondly, but there was a warning note to it.

"Tetchy creatures, minks," contributed Uncle Bertrand. "Now what you want is good English wool. None of that slippery foreign fur."

Mrs. Ramsby looked like she had bitten into a bad piece of toffee. "And this is your uncle," she enunciated. Without waiting for a response, she looked to Richard, "However did you contrive to, er, meet her?"

Amy clasped her hands together and looked soulful. "It was a dark and stormy night," she began.

She could hear Jane stifle a chuckle behind her.

It was true, as far as it went. It had been a dark and stormy night on a packet bound from Dover to Calais. Sometimes, truth could be stranger than fiction.

"We met while my wife was visiting her brother," said Richard repressively. That was true enough, too, but much less entertaining. It left out all the colorful bits.

Lady Jerard was as sweet as her mother was sour, but she put Amy's teeth on edge just as badly. "Does your brother live near here?" she inquired innocently. "Might I know him?"

"I don't think you would want to," said Amy. "He's a great disappointment as a sibling. Aside from being the means of my meeting Richard, of course."

She flung in an extra simper, just for good measure.

Richard sent her a quelling look. "Shall I fetch you something to eat?" he said, just a little too jovially.

"Reputation, lightly sautéed?" Amy muttered under her breath.

Her husband looked down at her with a wry expression, "Stewed, more likely. Or boiled. We are in England, after all."

She didn't need to be reminded of that. But for her, he wouldn't be. "I know," said Amy miserably. "I know."

Two long lines dented Richard's forehead as he looked down at her. So much for holiday cheer. "Amy—" he began.

But before he could get any farther, his mother swooped down on them, folding them both in a mince pie scented embrace.

Mince pie wasn't Lady Uppington's usual scent, but one of her grandchildren had already contrived to mash one against her green velvet bodice. As Lady Uppington said, it was all part of the joy of the season, and she had carried blithely on, mince pie, grandchild, and all. She seemed to have deposited Peregrine somewhere, but she was still wearing the mince pie.

Releasing her offspring, Lady Uppington beamed holiday cheer all around. "I do hope you're all enjoying yourselves."

From the determined look in her eye, it was quite clear that everyone was going to have a happy Christmas whether they liked it or not.

"Oh, very much so, Lady Uppington," piped up that puling pudding face of a Lady Jerard.

Hmm, Amy liked the alliteration of that. She rolled it a few times in her mind. Yes, even better with repetition.

Lady Uppington wafted her fan vaguely in the direction of her son's lost love. "Yes, yes," she said dismissively, "very good," before turning to radiate an extra measure of warmth in Amy's direction. "And how are *you*, my dear?" She smiled a butter-wouldn't-melt smile at Mrs. Ramsby and Lady Jerard. "They're only just married, you know. And so very, *very* happy."

Amy quickly straightened up and did her best to look very, very happy. She began to understand why Lady Uppington had invited Richard's lost love. From the expression on Richard's face as he looked down at the top of his mother's golden head, so did he.

One of his mother's green ostrich feathers poked him in the nose, and he sneezed.

"Bless you!" trilled Lady Uppington cheerfully, getting in an extra glare at Mrs. Ramsby for good measure. "You can't be getting sick now! Not when you're just *married*!"

Hell hath no fury like a mother whose son has been scorned, even when the scorning was a very long time ago.

Richard himself was remarkably silent. Amy glanced up at him, but he was smiled blandly at no one in particular, looking maddeningly urbane and diplomatic.

Uncle Bertrand dealt Lord Uppington a staggering whack on the shoulder. "Your sheep are looking much improved since the last time I visited them, Uppington. Much improved!"

With the consummate tact for which he was famed in diplomatic circles, Lord Uppington discreetly dodged a second whap, leaving Uncle Bertrand's hand to land harmlessly against the wall. "It must be that mash you recommended for them," he said kindly.

"Most like, most like," agreed Uncle Bertrand. "I sampled it meself. What's good enough for my little ones is good enough for me, I always say. Excellent stuff, that mash."

"I'm afraid we haven't any for supper tonight," Lady Uppington chimed in, the bobbing feathers on her headdress doing little to conceal the glint of mischief in her amused green eyes. "But it can be arranged if you so desire."

"Nah, nah," demurred Uncle Bertrand, visibly softened by his hostess' solicitude. "I shouldn't like to be a bother."

"Dear Mr. Wooliston," said Lady Uppington with the charm that had brought princes to their knees and made even that hardened ovine enthusiast blush, "you could never be a bother. We shall always be entirely in your debt for the pleasure your niece's presence in our family has afforded us."

"Niece..." It took Uncle Bertrand a moment to recall himself from his flocks. Lady Uppington put him in mind of an ewe he had once known. A charming one, she had been, with a jaunty curl to her fleece and a certain something to her eye.

Lady Uppington discreetly signaled with her fan.

Uncle Bertrand's eye cleared. "Oh, you mean our Amy! More of a daughter than a niece to me, she is," he said heartily, a sentiment that won him a warm smile of approval from Lady Uppington.

Amy could have told Lady Uppington that Uncle Bertrand meant exactly what he said. He couldn't remember his own daughters' names either. It was a matter of pure luck that he had managed to give the correct daughter away at her cousin Sophia's wedding.

"How very sweet," interjected Mrs. Ramsby, in a voice like a nutcracker snapping down on a particularly tough shell. "Such rustic simplicity.

Like something out of a comedy by Mr. Shakespeare. You have been to the theatre, haven't you, dear?"

Really! Just because she had been raised in Shropshire didn't mean she was a complete rustic. Somehow, it no longer seemed quite so amusing that Mrs. Ramsby appeared to have decided that she was a glorified sort of shepherdess, rescued by Richard from rural obscurity. Amy spared a moment to hope that Uncle Bertrand had left his sheep outside.

Was there some way to work into the conversation that her father could trace his lineage back to Charlemagne, or might that be considered tacky?

"I've been to the theatre both here and abroad," she said loftily. Ha! Let them compete with that. "My brother has a box in the Comedie Francais."

"Yes, but what does he keep in it?" said Lady Jerard in her soft voice, with a little smile to show that she was fooling.

"His own counsel," flashed back Amy. It didn't make much sense, but it was the first thing that came to mind. But, then, thought Amy mutinously, it was really Lady Jerard's fault for punning on boxes in the first place. So there. With knobs on.

"Can one really keep counsel in a box?"

Richard's former best friend and current brother-in-law, Miles Dorrington, strolled over to join them. He kept well on the other side of the grouping from Richard, though. Matters between them had been strained since Miles had married Henrietta, in a manner that could at best be termed precipitate.

"Deuced convenient, that. One could take it out when needed and bottle it away again when it became annoying."

Henrietta snatched a chunk of gingerbread out of her husband's fingers. "Like Pandora's box, only without all the nasty bits," she agreed. Taking a bite, she made a face and handed it back. "Too much orange peel."

"But if it didn't have any of the nasty bits," Miles said, absently cramming the rest of the gingerbread into his mouth, "it wouldn't be Pandora's box. It would be a different box."

"Why ever not?" countered Henrietta, cunningly waiting until Miles' mouth was full. "No one ever said Pandora couldn't reuse the box for other things once she had emptied it. It makes perfect sense to me."

It didn't to Miles, but his mouth was gummed together with gingerbread. "Mrrrr-mrrr-mrrr-mrr," he complained.

"Who," demanded Mrs. Ramsby, "is Pandora?"

"I should think one might call her a first cousin of Eve," said Lord Uppington mildly. "Excessively curious ladies, both."

Lady Uppington wrinkled her nose at him. "Come, come, Edward, don't tell me you wouldn't have eaten that apple."

"Only if you had offered it to me, my dear," replied Lord Uppington.

A loud groan emerged from Henrietta.

"They're flirting again," said Henrietta, in tragic tones.

She looked to her brother for support—it was his turn to express his horror—but Richard was a thousand miles away. Or maybe not miles, thought Amy, with a sinking feeling, but years away, back in the days when he was dashing around France with the sentimental memory of the fine eyes of one Miss Deirdre Ramsby to lend him inspiration.

That same former Miss Ramsby blinked her wide blue eyes at Amy. In a voice of innocent confusion, Lady Jerard asked, "How does your brother come to have a box at the Comedie Francaise?" She spoke the French words with decided discomfort. "Isn't the Comedie Francaise in France?"

No, it's in Hertfordshire.

"Yes," Amy replied, so demurely that Jane sent a sharp glance in her direction. "My brother resides in France. It would make little sense for him to have a box at a theatre in any other place."

Mrs. Ramsby looked at her sharply. "Whatever does he do there?"

"Go to the theatre, one assumes," provided Miles blithely. "Ouch!"

"That," said Miss Gwen gravely, "was for being impertinent."

"I thought it was very pertinent," muttered Miles, but he made sure to stay well out of range of Miss Gwen's fan as he said it. "I say, Hen, do you have any more gingerbread?"

Mrs. Ramsby was still attempting to conquer her natural revulsion at the notion of the foreign capital. The French were worse than sheep. Sheep…. French brothers…. Wherever *had* Lord Richard found that woman?

29

"Did you spend a great deal of time among the French, then, Lady Richard?" The title seemed to come hard to the older woman's tongue.

Well, let it, thought Amy belligerently. Her daughter had had the opportunity to own it and had turned it down to marry her elderly baron, trading a mere courtesy title for a peerage as though the exchange of one man for another were nothing more than a move on a chess board, so many points to be won. Amy had never valued the worth of a man at his place in the peerage. She had seen for herself that it brought danger as well as privilege. Richard's worth lay in himself.

Most of the time.

Amy snaked a glance at her oblivious husband. What was he thinking leaving her to the wolves like this? Not that she needed rescuing, of course. She could very well rescue herself. But, *still*. Did he not want to take up cudgels against his former love? It was very hard to fight against the phantom of What Might Have Been.

"I was born in Paris," Amy replied. "And spent my early youth there. My father was French. I am half-French."

From the expression on Mrs. Ramsby's face, she clearly felt that that explained a great deal.

"You must find France sadly changed," ventured Lady Jerard, in the tone of one determined to smooth oil over troubled waters, whether the waters wished to be oiled or not.

Why did the vile Deirdre have to be so… pleasant? It was very irritating. Amy took it as a personal offense.

"Change," broke in Miss Gwen, in her precise, clipped accents, "is distinctly overrated. It is so seldom managed properly."

"Change?" bellowed Uncle Bertrand. "What's this about change? I don't hold with it! In my day, we thought it sufficient to change our linen three times a year, and that was change enough for us."

Across the room, Amy's cousin Agnes, who had been glowing with the thrill of her first grown-up party, looked about ready to sink beneath the settee. Amy knew how she felt.

"But, Bertrand, dear," piped up Aunt Prudence, in her vague, gentle voice, blinking her nearsighted eyes at him, "we've talked about that."

Uncle Bertrand deflated, his chin sinking into the folds of his cravat. While much wrinkled, it had clearly been washed within the fortnight.

"Yes, I know," he mumbled, before rousing himself sufficiently to add, with a hint of belligerence, "Not that I see aught wrong with a peck or two of good English dirt! If it's good enough for England, it's good enough for me!"

Lady Uppington's lips twitched. "There's something to be said for good English water, too," she said tactfully.

"Aye, in its place," agreed Uncle Bertrand, determined to make himself agreeable to his hostess.

"Streams?" suggested Miles. "Rivers? Duck ponds? Eeep!"

His wife smiled sweetly at him. "You've been in that duck pond before. Don't make me put you there again."

Miles folded his arms across his chest. "I'll have you know that I'm quite fond of ducks."

"Yes, on a plate," retorted his wife. "When they can't peck back."

Amy was used to their banter by now. Ignoring them, she looked to her own husband, who was rubbing his head as though he had the headache.

"Are you unwell?" Amy whispered.

Richard shook his head, like a swimmer breaking through the water. "I just need a breath of air. You'll be all right?"

"Of course," said Amy.

Ignoring the swirl of conversation around her, she watched as her husband gracefully extricated himself the grouping. Fending off his mother's concerns about his health, he slipped out of the room, moving with all the speed of a man trying to outpace his own private pack of demons.

Amy just wished it didn't feel quite so much as though he were running away from her.

CHAPTER THREE

I saw three ships come sailing in,
On Christmas Day, on Christmas Day,
I saw three ships come sailing in,
On Christmas Day in the morning.

And what was in those ships all three?
    -- "I Saw Three Ships"

The air was cooler in the hallway, away from the pressing heat of too many people, too many candles, and too much hot food all crammed into the same space. Funny, how even a room the size of a village green could feel crammed with enough people stuffed into it.

That wasn't it, though, was it? It wasn't the number of people or the smell of the food or the glare of the candles. It was the expression on Amy's face when she had made that comment about being stranded in England. Richard couldn't remember the exact phrasing of it, but the meaning had been clear enough.

It was maddening to know what she wanted and to be incapable of doing anything at all about it.

Only that wasn't quite honest, was it? He could do something about it. That was the worst of it. In the back of his mind lurked the niggling possibility that if Amy really wanted to go back to France, it could be arranged. The only person who knew of her complicity in his escape was the Assistant to the Minister of Police, and he had since been retired to a private institution on the outskirts of Paris—for a rest, as the official report went. Absolutely barking barmy, was the way Richard's source had put it. With Delaroche out of the way, Amy's path would be clear.

Or it would have been, if she hadn't married him. Marriage to the former Purple Gentian was a sure way to blight the career of a budding spy.

Even so, she might manage it. Her brother was well-liked in Bonaparte's court, her cousin received without a qualm. There were few people in Paris who would recognize her. She could pose as a cousin, a maid, anything she liked, rather than staying in rural seclusion in Sussex, yoked to a useless former member of His Majesty's secret service, with nothing better to do than tell over the tales of his aging exploits by the crackle of the winter fire.

Richard's head thudded painfully.

It took him a moment to realize the noise wasn't entirely coming from inside his own skull. Heavy footfalls reverberated along the marble passageway behind him as a very large object propelled itself down the hallway with a vigor that made the statues shake in their niches.

"I say! Hold up a moment!" Richard's one-time best friend came skidding to a halt beside Richard.

Not one-time. Long-time. He and Miles had been inseparable from Eton on, until Miles had had the temerity to marry Richard's sister. Yet another upheaval in a year of upheavals.

It had been pointed out to Richard, forcibly and repeatedly, by the various females in his family, that the choice had not been entirely Miles'. Henrietta had had a hand in it, too.

But it had still felt like a betrayal. A betrayal of whom, of what, and of why was not something that Richard felt like examining too closely. He had clung stubbornly to the mantra that Miles Should Have Known Better.

"Known better than whom?" his mother had said, with a pointed look at him.

That just made it worse. Just which one of them was her actual offspring? Miles might have been practically part of the family, but he was only so because Richard had brought him home, like a stray dog found begging at the kitchen door. He was supposed to be Richard's dog—well, friend.

At the moment, he looked more like a kicked dog, gearing up to dodge another blow. As he trotted along beside, Richard could see Miles watching him warily, gearing up for yet another rebuff. He had been administering a lot of those recently, hadn't he?

"Don't look like that," said Richard irritably. He hadn't meant to say it irritably. It was just that everything seemed to come out that way these days. "I'm not going to bite."

"A fine way you have of showing it," Miles said, rolling his eyes in an exaggerated way, but there was too much truth in it for it to be entirely in fun.

It made Richard want to lower his head in his hands and groan. A fine mess he had made of things, hadn't he? His wife unhappy, his best friend afraid of him.... Could he take the hands of the clock, turn them back, and do it all over again, starting somewhere back last Christmas?

"I'm sorry," he said, instead, not meeting his old friend's eyes as he pushed open the door to one of the smaller book rooms. There were three of them in Uppington Hall, in gradations of grandness. Richard had deliberately chosen the least grand, the one his father tended to use the most.

Richard went unerringly to the cabinet where the port was kept, drawing out a decanter and two glasses. He had been raiding the decanter in this particular study since he had turned twelve. Richard pulled out the stopper, filling each glass half full of ruby liquid, the finest product of Oporto. Funny, how some things stayed the same, while other things turned inside out and upside down.

Sometimes, Richard felt as though the world had chosen 1803 to turn on its head and spin like a top, with nothing to do but to cling to the sides and hope that it eventually would all turn right side up.

Shrugging, he handed Miles a glass. "It's been a strange year."

"At least it's almost over!" Miles said cheerfully, seizing eagerly at the olive branch, pathetic and puny one though it was. He raised his glass in an impromptu toast. "Here's to 1804! Mmm, port," he added happily, smacking his lips. "Nice port, too."

Richard's lips twisted, despite himself. He'd missed Miles. He didn't like to admit it, but he had.

But all he said was, "Let's hope a good wine makes a good year."

Miles grinned as he plopped himself down in a Jacobean cane chair. "It can't hurt."

"Yes, it can," said Richard dryly. "The next morning."

Miles looked at him warily, as though suspecting a dangerous double meaning, but said, easily enough, "Time enough to think about that then." He waved a hand airily through the air. "Sufficient unto the day, and all that—urgh!"

The hand, unfortunately, had been the one holding his glass.

"I hate to be the one to tell you this," said Richard, nodding at the puddle of crimson liquid sinking nicely into the tan buckskin of Miles' breeches, "but port is meant to be ingested through the lips, not the leg. Just something you might want to know."

"Oh, ha bloody ha." Removing a handkerchief from his sleeve, Miles scrubbed at the stain, succeeding only in spreading it across a wider area. Richard couldn't fail to notice that the handkerchief had been unevenly embroidered with Miles' initials. Or, rather, initial. The placement of the single, wobbly "M" suggested that it had initially been planned as part of a larger grouping.

"Henrietta embroider you handkerchiefs, did she?" said Richard, nodding at the scrap of cloth.

Stopping mid-scrub, Miles grinned fondly at the now reddened scrap. "Well, handkerchief, really. The others are still in progress."

"Ah, yes," said Richard cynically. "I still have the slipper Henrietta gave me for my birthday last year. When I asked her where the other one was, she told me it would be good for my health to hop."

Miles beamed proudly. "She does like to get the last word. Jolly long ones, too, most of the time."

Something about the glow on his old friend's face suddenly made Richard feel very, very small.

He looked down into his own port, and saw only the wobbly reflection of his own face, darkened and distorted by the effect of light on liquid. If they were happy, who was he to object? Not that he hadn't had cause, back in June, he told himself, when he had found his best friend and sister together in an extremely compromising position. But if Miles really loved her....

The force of Richard's exhalation made ripples across the surface of the liquid, wrinkling his reflected face into a dozen identical folds.

"Look," he said gruffly, by way of preamble.

Miles obediently looked. Henrietta had always said that Miles was excellent with direct commands. The recollection made Richard wince, but he continued doggedly on, nonetheless. It was Christmas, devil take it, and he was bloody well going to be noble if it killed him.

It did occur to him that there might be something a little self-defeating about framing the sentiment in that way, but he dismissed that as beside the point.

Richard cleared his throat. It was the port, of course. Bloody viscous stuff, port. "Look," he repeated. "Shall we let bygones be? New year, new leaf?"

Miles grinned at him, an all out grin that all but split his face in half. "I don't see any bygones here, do you?"

Richard could. They were all around him, like evil sprites. Lost friends, lost opportunities, lost causes. "No," he said. "Not a one."

"Excellent." Miles rubbed his hands together, flinging himself back across his chair with an unaffected exuberance that seriously taxed the capabilities of the two hundred year old frame. "There's something I've been wanting to run by you, something that came across my desk at the War Office...."

Stretching his legs out in front of him, Richard permitted himself a groan. The port must be mellowing him. "I miss the War Office."

"They miss you, too," said Miles sympathetically, before getting down to business. "Do you know a Captain Wright?"

"With an arr or a double-u?"

Miles did some quick mental spelling. No one watching him would ever have been able to guess that he had been top of their class at Eton for classical Greek.

Triumphantly shaking back the hair from his brow, Miles announced, "Both."

"Has a boat, hasn't he?" recalled Richard.

Miles was generous enough not to point out that the word "captain" generally implied the possession of some form of nautical conveyance.

It was beginning to come back. "Captain John Wright? He's a naval man. He carried the odd packet back to England for me, when I couldn't get hold of another means of convoy."

Miles nodded. "He's carrying more than correspondence these days. There's a rumor than he's been smuggling émigrés back into France."

"What kind of émigrés?"

Miles flopped back in his chair. "That's the devil of it. We don't know. They might just be simple souls yearning for home and hearth. Or...."

That "or" carried a multitude of possibilities, most of them dangerous. All of Richard's old instincts twanged discordantly. If Captain Wright was smuggling across French émigrés intent on fomenting revolution against the revolution, their amateur bumblings might do more harm to the royalist cause than—well, than any number of Bonaparte's canons. The last thing they needed was another failed Royalist coup to give Bonaparte an excuse to tighten security and call public sympathy to his side.

If that was the case, something would have to be done immediately to neutralize the amateur plotters. They would have to—

Richard caught himself up short. They. Not he. He had nothing to do with it anymore. He had been retired. Rusticated. It was Jane Wooliston's business now. The Purple Gentian had left the garden.

Richard took a long swig of his port before speaking. "Why tell me? I'm out of commission these days." He could feel himself wallowing. Surely, a little wallow was permissible, on an occasion such as this.

"Only in France," said Miles helpfully.

"If you'll forgive me pointing out the obvious," Richard said sarcastically, leaning over to splash a second round of port into Miles' glass before topping up his own, "France just happens to be where the enemy is."

"That doesn't mean there isn't work to be done here. Some of us never got to go romp around France in a black mask in the first place."

"Do you expect me to feel sorry for you?" Richard tossed back, setting the stopper firmly in the decanter.

"No." Something in Miles' voice made Richard's hand still on the stopper. It was perfectly cheerful, but…. Richard looked up from the decanter and met his old friend's guileless brown eyes. "No more than I do for you."

"Hmph," said Richard.

Miles played the buffoon so well, it was easy to forget that he was generally brighter than he let on. He was bright enough not to spoil his advantage by pressing it home. Instead, he said cheerfully, "You still have connections among the émigré community in London, haven't you? And on the coast?"

Not entirely recent ones, but…. "Yes," he said guardedly.

"Excellent! Once Christmas is over—"

He broke off as Richard abruptly held up a hand. What was that? Old instincts died hard. He had acted before he had even fully identified the noise. There had been a creaking sound, like a floorboard, or a door hinge.

"Is anyone there?" he called out sharply.

His instincts were rewarded. The door swung slowly inward, revealing the figure of a woman, her hair drawn into curls at the sides, held up by violet flowers that matched the color of her half-mourning.

"I'm so sorry," said Deirdre. No, not Deirdre, Richard reminded himself. Lady Jerard. "I do hope I'm not interrupting."

Both gentlemen rose hastily to their feet.

"Not at all," said Richard smoothly.

Miles made a grunting noise that just barely passed for assent, but the expression on his face couldn't be mistaken for anything other than hostility, iced over with a fragile veneer of good manners. He nodded generally in Deirdre's direction, without ever looking directly at her.

Miles had never forgiven Deirdre for Tony.

"I should be getting back," Miles said, brushing his hands vigorously against his thighs, as though scrubbing off something unpleasant.

Richard suppressed a sigh, feeling all the fatigue of the day descending upon him. He didn't particularly want to deal with Deirdre either, but his reasons weren't quite the same as Miles'. When he looked at Deirdre, he didn't see her crime. He saw his. He had been young and foolish and desperate to impress the object of his infatuation. It had been his indiscretion, boasting to Deirdre of their plans in

France, that had led to Tony's death. Why should Deirdre have suspected her maid of being a French spy? That had been his responsibility, not hers, and he had failed.

The only crime Deirdre had committed was in choosing Baron Jerard over him, and that was a crime he could easily forgive, although at the time, it had felt like capital treason. Now, years removed, it was hard to remember why. Oh, she was certainly easy on the eyes—she still was, at that—but there had never been anything more. All his memories were of long looks, of worshipful silences, of his own voice singing her praises. They must have conversed, but he couldn't recall a single conversation worth remembering. When it came down to it, they had never really had anything to say to each other.

That was not a problem from which he and Amy could be said to suffer.

He really ought to get back to the drawing room and Amy. But there was Deirdre to be dealt with. He did feel that he owed her something, after all these years. She had been his first love, even if a hollow one, and one didn't dismiss that lightly.

Richard forced a pleasant smile onto his face, and said, "Were you looking for me?" Given their history, that hadn't come out quite right. He modified it to, "Might I help you?"

Deirdre's eyes scanned the room, as though searching for something she had lost, before settling, sadly, on him. "You might have. Once."

Richard could hear the chime of silvery bells in his brain. Warning bells.

Before he could get too alarmed, Deirdre shook her head, holding up her hands in a charming gesture of abnegation. "Don't mind me," she said ruefully. She glanced down at the bulbous sapphire ring that still circled her finger, Baron Jerard's betrothal ring. "It has been a difficult season."

"At least you had several good years together," said Richard awkwardly. It did feel a bit bizarre to be belatedly consoling her for the death of the man for whom she had jilted him. But he felt, in retrospect, more than a little bit grateful to Baron Jerard. Who knows, he thought generously. Perhaps Deirdre had genuinely loved the man, for all that he was sixty if he was a day.

"Several years, yes." Deirdre stared down into the depths of her sapphire as though it were an oracle and might speak to her. "Good years?" She shook her head slowly in unspoken condemnation of her late husband.

Bloody, bloody, bloody blast. This was the last thing he needed, to play father confessor to outworn infatuation.

"I'm very sorry to hear that," he said, for lack of anything better.

His half-hearted words made more of an impression than he had intended. Deirdre roamed idly around the room, her ruffled flounce making a muted swishing sound, like snow shifting in tree branches.

She braced her hands against the edge of Robert's father's desk. Her head bowed, she said, "There is something I have wanted to say to you for a very long time, something long overdue."

"If it is that overdue," suggested Richard gently, trying very hard not to glance at the clock on the mantle as he said it, "perhaps, then, it is better not said at all."

"How like you," murmured Deirdre, "to try to spare me pain."

Well, no. Once upon a time, he had wished her a good deal of pain. Once upon a time, he had also written a vast quantity of very mawkish poetry, comparing her eyes to pansies sprinkled with morning dew, and her teeth to peerless pearls. Or was it her skin that had been peerless pearl? One forgot, after all these years. Richard tried to imagine how Amy would react were he to address something of the kind to her. Hooting sounds of laughter seemed the most likely response.

He nearly betrayed himself into a grin, but the somber expression on Deirdre's face caught him up short just in time.

Poor woman; they had both suffered from their brief affair. They had both lost the dream of what might have been between them. He, at least, had had the luxury of resenting her for it. He had fumed and come to terms and found someone, in the end, who suited him a hundred times better, not in an illusion of romantic love, but in the rough and tumble of the workaday thing. She, on the other hand, had borne the burden of having made the decision, with nothing to show for it in the end but an empty title and an emptier bed. He could find it in himself to feel sorry for her. Now.

Deirdre looked at him long and earnestly. "I am sorry that it ended... as it did."

It was a compliment, of a sort. "Thank you," said Richard gravely.

What time *was* it? Long past time to be getting back to the drawing room. Unfortunately, Deirdre didn't seem to be done yet. She held out one gloved hand to him.

"I never meant to hurt you." Candlelight glinted off her curls as she bowed her head in remembered pain. "I never meant to hurt anyone."

Poor consolation for Tony, dead these six years.

But there was no point in recriminations. Deirdre had been careless, not malicious. In his hurt and resentment, it had been easy to forget that she must suffer Tony on her conscience, just as he did.

"Of course, you didn't," said Richard, all manly solicitude. "Let's say nothing more about it."

"I hope…" she began falteringly, stopped, and tried again. "I hope that I was not the end of your operations abroad. So much good to be stopped for so little."

Her mathematical skills never had been much to talk about, had they? His unmasking in the press—and, more importantly, in Bonaparte's files—had occurred last spring; Deirdre's role in his life had ended seven years ago. There was a slight time lag there.

"Think nothing of it," he said gallantly. At least, it might have been gallant if he hadn't meant it quite literally. There really was nothing to think of there.

"Do you mean… that is…" her voice dropped to a breathy whisper. "Are you still carrying on your work, despite it all?"

Richard felt as though he were stuck in a curious sort of gap in time. If they had to have this conversation, shouldn't it have been seven years ago? It was entirely irrelevant now. Unless, he thought, she was still caught in the net she had woven for herself, even though, to him, those were all as events from another lifetime.

He much preferred this lifetime, he realized— even if it did mean a cessation of those cross-Channel activities that even Deirdre's accidental meddling had failed to end.

Kindly, but firmly, he said, "Whatever passed between us was over long, long ago. Your conscience should have no qualms about it."

"How noble you are," she said sadly. "How good! If I had known then one half of what I know now…. Oh, Richard!"

"Well!" said Richard heartily, beating a hasty retreat to the window. "Just look at that snow!"

Thank goodness for the weather. It was always there, always a proper topic of conversation. Nothing forestalled inconvenient displays of emotion quite like a disquisition on climatic conditions.

"Oh dear," said Deirdre softly. Richard had once dotingly termed that tone "dulcet". In his new lexicon, Richard re-labeled it "bloody hard to hear properly". "It is coming down."

"That is what snow does," Richard agreed, moving purposefully towards the study door. "Shall I show you and your mother to your carriage? You must want to get a start on the drive."

Deirdre remained remarkably stationary. She looked up at him from under her lashes.

"Our coachman doesn't like driving in the snow...."

CHAPTER FOUR

The holly bears a berry, as red as any blood....
The holly bears a prickle, as sharp as any thorn....
The holly bears a bark, as bitter as any gall....
    -- "The Holly and the Ivy"

"You invited her to stay?"

"It's just for the one night." Richard added defensively, "Their coachman doesn't like to drive in the snow."

"Oh, for heaven's sake!"

It didn't help that Richard agreed with her. "Well, what I was supposed to do?" he asked testily. "Fling Deirdre and her aged mother out into the snow?"

The use of his former beloved's Christian name had been a tactical error. He could see it in the narrowing of Amy's blue eyes.

"No," she said with dangerous calm. "You were supposed to fling them into their carriage, which is

49

designed to ride *through* the snow. That's what carriages are for."

Richard scrubbed a hand through his hair. "Not this one apparently." Letting his breath out in a long sigh, he looped an arm around Amy's shoulders, pulling her against him. "Why all the fuss? If we were back at Selwick Hall, you would do the same for any other guest who didn't want to travel. There's certainly room enough in this old pile."

Amy shrugged out of his embrace. "I don't like the way she forced her way in."

"She didn't exactly batter down the castle gates," Richard retorted. "My mother invited her."

Amy made a grand, sweeping gesture. "Oh, and if your mother invited her, then it must be all right."

"What is that supposed to mean?" From the look on Amy's face, she didn't know either, but she wasn't about to admit it. Richard pressed his eyes shut. He wished he knew exactly what they were fighting about. Or was it just that they were clearly bound to fight about something? His two glasses of port—or had it been three—were beginning to catch up with him in a bad way. "Look. There was no way my mother could have not invited Deirdre. She's a neighbor. We've always held open house at Uppington Hall on Christmas Eve."

Amy folded her arms across her chest. "Of course. And she's a part of that world."

Richard had a feeling he was about to step into something soft and squishy, but he ventured forward anyway. "Yes."

"And I'm not."

Ah. That was the squishy bit. "I didn't say that."

Shaking her head, Amy turned away. "Never mind. I'm just— Never mind."

Concerned, Richard followed after her, resting his hands on her shoulders. "Just what?" he asked.

He could see the bared nape of her neck as she bent her head forward, the little tendrils of curl escaping from their ribbon dark against the tender skin. Ordinarily, he would have kissed her curls away, but this didn't seem a moment for that.

Amy gave a little shake of her head. Richard could feel her shoulders rise and fall beneath his hands as she shrugged. "Nothing," she said, turning jerkily, so that she was addressing the top button of his waistcoat. "Just—all this. Seeing Jane. Too much mince pie."

"It's not the mince pie, is it?" Richard asked grimly. "It's the Jane bit."

Amy lifted her head. Her eyes looked darker than usual, too dark in the shadow cast by his body. Richard thought abstractedly that this was the second pair of big, soulful blue eyes he had encountered this evening in this very same room. But this time, there was a difference. He cared.

"A little," she admitted. "No. A lot."

Richard felt a lump in his chest that was more than just the three pieces of mince pie he had shared with his nephew. Out of the mass of indigestible emotion, he found himself blurting out, "If you had it all to do again, would you do it differently?"

Amy took a step back. Someone, presumably his niece Caroline, had stuck a sprig of holly into the bandeau that held back her curls. It had come unmoored, bobbing drunkenly beside one ear, like a buoy in a deserted sea.

"Do what?" she asked warily.

Grimacing, Richard made an abortive gesture. "All this. You had so little time over there before we had to leave—before I had to leave," he corrected. He, at least, had had seven years playing hero, long enough, if he were being entirely honest, for the exercise to begin to stale. Amy, on the other hand, had had three months, three months after a lifetime of training. "Are you sorry?"

"Sorry?"

Richard tried to keep his voice light. "That you yoked your lot to mine."

Amy plucked the sprig of holly from behind her ear, squinted at it, made a face, and tossed it onto the desk. "I don't usually think of it as a yoke."

Richard didn't like the sound of that "usually". "Just when Jane comes to visit, then."

Amy sketched an impatient gesture that could equally be taken as negation, assent, or do-we-really-have-to-talk-about-this-now? "We should be getting back," she said. "Your mother wanted to get up a game of charades."

"Bother the chara—"

"*And* you have house guests now."

Richard cursed bloody Deirdre, her bloody mother, and their bloody coachman to perdition. He threw in the snow for good measure while he was at it. Bother the snow.

"I had house guests before," muttered Richard. "And they aren't my guests, they're my parents' guests."

Amy dignified that with all the response it deserved. None. Tucking her holly more firmly into her hair, she swept the train of her red velvet dress up over her arm and started for the door, back towards charades, and house guests, and assorted dotty relatives who would effectively preclude their having any sort of meaningful conversation just by being themselves. Not that he was doing too well on the conversation front as it was—digging his own grave appeared to be the operative phrase—but he couldn't let her go off looking like that. Not when it lay within his power to fix it.

"Wait—" Richard caught his wife by the hand. She looked back over her shoulder. A holly berry gave up its hold on her hair ornament and jounced off her shoulder before rolling harmlessly to the carpet. Before Richard could allow himself to think better of it, he took a very deep breath, and rattled off, all at once, "Would-you-like-to-go-back-to-France?"

Amy dropped her train in her surprise. The heavy fabric slid to the ground with a swish like falling snow. "What?"

"When Jane goes back, you could, too. It would be tricky"—Richard paused, fighting the impulse to enumerate and multiply the trickiness until it moved from tricky into impossible—"but it could be done," he finished nobly. "You can still do what you always wanted to do."

Without him.

That part appeared to have occurred to Amy, too. "And what about you?"

Richard shrugged. "Miles seems to think that there's work to be done on this end."

The idea didn't hold much savor at the moment. Going back to an empty house to code dispatches at the end of the day struck him as immeasurably lonely. He'd got used to being part of a pair. Being by himself would feel like being—well, holly without the ivy. Mince without the pie. Something less than the sum of its parts.

Amy slowly gathered up the fabric of her train, pleating it up bit by little bit, with slow movements entirely unlike her usual self. "So I would go back to France and you would stay here."

No, he wanted to say. *Out of the question.* But having broached the possibility, he couldn't snatch it away again. There were nasty names for people who offered gifts and then took them back.

"It is a possibility," he said, as neutrally as he could. "Think about it. Decide what you want."

Amy looked at him sideways, her brows drawing together over her nose. "What do *you* want?"

That was easy enough. For both of them to be in France again, swinging through windows on ropes, leaving mocking notes on pillows, and spiriting men out of prison, together.

Oh, hell. He didn't even need France. It was the together bit that counted. He would settle for being back at Selwick Hall, pre-Christmas, pre-Deirdre, setting up their spy school and arguing over the best route from Calais to Paris.

He took refuge in banalities. "For you to be happy."

"On the opposite side of the Channel?"

I could not love thee dear so much, loved I not honor more.... It had always been one of his favorite

54

verses. Why should it be only the woman who waited, while the man went adventuring? The sentiment applied both ways.

"If that's what it takes," he said grimly. That hadn't come out quite right, had it? This whole waving from the castle portcullis thing might be harder than he had thought. Pinning his face into a great, big, fake smile, Richard said with exaggerated heartiness, "Think about it. Consider it... a Christmas gift."

"Thank you." Amy's voice was curiously subdued, her face shadowed by that absurd sprig of greenery. Shouldn't she be... happier? Excited? Relieved? Richard frowned, trying to see around the spiky leaves. "I will."

Richard's eyes followed his wife's progress as she strode out of the room. He was trying to read the set of her back. It told him nothing more than that her dress appeared to have even more than the usual number of buttons and that if the set of her shoulders was anything to go by, he wasn't going to be the one undoing them. He had blundered and he wasn't quite sure how.

Wasn't that what she wanted? To have the chance to go back to France?

Bloody snow. Bloody Deirdre. Bloody, bloody, bloody Christmas. He knew he should have just given her a kitten.

Richard realized, belatedly and unhelpfully, just how much he had counted on an immediate denial. She was supposed to elated, tearful, thankful—and then say no. "No, dearest," said a ridiculous falsetto in his head. "Never mind the espionage. My place is here with you." Cue embracing. And so forth. He got to be all noble, she said no, and they all lived happily ever after.

Instead... Richard buried his head in his hands. What the devil was he to do when she actually took him up on his offer?

*   *   *

The holly was bobbing loose against her cheek again.

Plucking it out, Amy let it drop onto one of the small tables that littered the hallway. She wasn't feeling terribly festive at the moment. In the space of five minutes, the entire holiday had gone as rancid as last year's Christmas pudding.

It couldn't be a good thing when one's husband of nine months started suggesting cross-Channel living arrangements.

There was a cold breeze in the center hall, snaking under the heavily carved panels of the front door, whistling around the corners of the windows, lurking beneath the great curved dome of a ceiling that soared three stories above. The greenery Lady Uppington had draped across every available surface ought to have leant warmth to the space but the vast proportions of the chamber seemed to dwarf all human efforts. Amy pulled her shawl closer around her shoulders.

There was someone else in the hall, blending neatly into the wall. It was Jane, holding a creased piece of paper close by one of the tall branches of candles that lit the hall.

"What are you reading?" Amy asked, crossing the hall to her cousin.

"Just some… verse," said Jane abstractedly.

"Verse?" It was Mrs. Ramsby, standing in the open door of the receiving room.

In a moment, Jane had gone from an accomplished operative to a blushing debutante. The transformation was astounding. A gentle flush stained her perfect porcelain cheeks as she modestly lowered her eyelashes. "Just—just a poem," she faltered, the picture of maidenly guilt. "From a friend."

Pat on her cue, Miss Gwen stalked out from behind Mrs. Ramsby. "A gentleman friend, no doubt," she snarled. "Give it here."

Jane pressed the scrap of paper to her chest, looking imploringly at her chaperone.

Miss Gwen extended her hand.

Reluctantly, clinging to the paper until the last moment, Jane surrendered the forbidden token to her chaperone.

It was, thought Amy, better than the dumb show in *Hamlet*, and far better acted than most theatricals she had seen, even at the Comedie Francaise.

"One of those London bucks, I shouldn't wonder," snapped Miss Gwen, reveling in her role. "Hmph!"

"It's just a poem," offered Amy, doing her best to play along, but something about the smoothness of the interplay between Jane and Miss Gwen made her feel like a grain of sand that had somehow got into a well-oiled clockwork.

Miss Gwen turned the full force of her glower on her former charge. "Poems today, love letters tomorrow. Don't think I've forgotten your example, missy!"

"Hullo! What's everyone doing out here?" Henrietta poked her head around the door, followed by Lady Jerard. Amy could have hugged her. Henrietta, that was. Not Lady Jerard. "Don't worry. You're not missing anything at charades. Miles is being a glass elephant again."

An indignant howl came from within the reception room. "They hadn't guessed it yet!" echoed hollowly through the hall.

"They were going to!" Henrietta tossed back blithely over her shoulder. "He's always a glass elephant. What's the entertainment out here? Mummers? Morris dancers?"

"Poetry," offered Amy.

"Oh," breathed Lady Jerard. "Did Richard write you poetry, too? I mean—oh dear, I shouldn't have said that, should I?"

Amy tossed her head. "I've always preferred prose."

"You mean he didn't write you any poetry," cackled Miss Gwen.

"I think I'm going to watch Miles be a glass elephant," said Henrietta loudly. "Who wants to join me?"

Everyone, apparently. Amy watched as Henrietta expertly shooed the straying guests back into the reception room. It was a useful skill for a hostess to have, guest herding. As they trooped back into the room, she could hear Miss Gwen's voice raised in strong disapproval of any pachyderm with the poor sense to choose such a fragile material as glass. "Entirely impractical!"

Amy lingered behind, waiting until Henrietta had signaled the footmen to close the twin door behind them before sidling over to Jane's side.

"What was it really?" Amy asked. "Before Miss Gwen appropriated it?"

"Better Miss Gwen than someone else." Jane's brows pulled together, creating two small, perfect furrows. Even Jane's worry lines were symmetrical. Amy could feel her own hair sticking up on one side where she had pulled out the holly, and hastily shoved it back under the bandeau. "It was a message. From Augustus. In verse," she added, with a hint of a smile.

Augustus Whittlesby had carefully cultivated his reputation as the most prolific poet in France, author of verse so bad that even Bonaparte's secret police thought twice before trying to slog through it.

So it was Augustus now, was it? Amy had long had her suspicions that Whittlesby's attentions were more than professional. But Jane didn't look like a woman who had just received a love letter.

Jane frowned. "It was foolhardy of him to send it to me here."

"It is in code, isn't it? In verse."

"I believe we clarified that already," said Jane dryly. "Oughtn't you to be enjoying the charades?"

"I don't like glass elephants." Now would be the time to tell Jane that she was free to join her in France. But Amy balked. Instead, she found herself blurting out. "Have you heard that the lovely Lady Jerard is staying the night?"

Jane delicately raised her brows. "The same lovely Lady Jerard who used to receive poetry from your husband?"

Amy bared her teeth. "That is the one."

"I don't think you really have anything to worry about," said Jane kindly.

Why was it that being told not to worry made one more inclined to do so? "Of course I'm not worried," Amy lied stoutly. And she wasn't. Not really. Not about that.

"I'm surprised Lady Uppington invited her," Jane said thoughtfully, digging the hole deeper. "Given her history."

Amy didn't ask how Jane knew. Jane knew everything. Always had done, always would. There were times when it came in quite handy. At other times it was unspeakably infuriating. Fortunately, this was one of the former. The fewer explanations she needed to make, the better.

"I think she wanted to gloat," said Amy frankly. "Over Richard being all settled. Besides, it was just her maid who was the French spy."

"And her maid was dismissed," Jane mused.

"Well, yes. One would assume so."

"She was." Jane sounded quite definitive about it. "Without references."

Sometimes, Jane had the most irritating way of getting caught up in inconsequentialities. "What sort of references would one give? Excellent at cleaning linen, eavesdropping, and general mayhem?"

Jane gave Amy one of her patient looks. "Which meant that no one was able to track her down after… the incident. She simply disappeared."

"Back to France, presumably." Amy couldn't have cared less about the loathsome Deirdre's former maid.

To be fair, Deirdre wasn't even so loathsome. She was just generally insipid. When it came down to it, Amy wasn't even really jealous of her. Richard wasn't the sort to pine after lost loves. Lost careers, on the other hand….

On the whole, Amy would far rather the problem were Lady Jerard. One could compete against another woman. One couldn't compete against a lost way of life, especially when one was the direct cause of the losing of it.

"Oh, drat it all," Amy said belligerently, starting across the hall. Even glass elephants were preferable to the unpleasant gyre of her own thoughts. And maybe she could find Peregrine and get him to mash some more mince pie against her dress. "It's Christmas Eve and I'm going to go play charades."

Jane regarded the drawing room doors with an abstracted expression on her face. "It may be a more interesting game than you think."

CHAPTER FIVE

Silent night, holy night,
All is calm, all is bright.
-- "Silent Night"

The room was quiet. Too quiet.

Amy flung out an arm and felt along the empty space next to her. The sheets were cold, the mattress smooth, not dented by the weight of a human form. Richard still hadn't come to bed.

If she went to France, the other side of the bed would always be cold.

That was another problem with an empty bed; there was too much space for thought to creep in. Never a good idea late at night. Groaning, Amy rubbed her face in the pillow before levering herself on an elbow to peer at the clock on the mantel. The fire had burned down, but there was just enough of a glow left to make out the faint shape of the hands of the clock, angled somewhere past three.

The snow had died down sometime after midnight, lending the landscape outside the draperies an eerie calm. The branches of the trees were stark and black beneath their white tracery, and the moon glinted blue-white off the frost-crisped snow. There were already tracks across the ground, the double dots left by deer and the longer, blurrier footprints left by their two legged peers, the gardeners and the gamekeepers.

Where was Richard? She had left him playing billiards with Miles, after Henrietta had made sure that the pointy sticks were going to be used entirely for hitting the balls and not each other. It wasn't like him to stay up so late. On the other hand, it also wasn't every day that he broached the possibility of her moving to the side of the Channel.

Did he want her to go, or was it simply that he believed that she wanted to go? Amy felt a twinge of guilt at the memory of all the times she had made careless comments about how unfair it was that he had got to spend seven years playing hero, while she had three measly months, all the times she had grimaced over the appearance of the Pink Carnation's name in the illustrated papers, or sighed over the atlases of places she might never see again.

But just because she said she wanted to go didn't mean she actually wanted to go—at least, not on those terms. Didn't Richard realize that? Oh, heavens, how did she expect him to make sense of it when she couldn't make sense of it herself?

It was useless! Amy flung back the covers. There was no point in even pretending to sleep. She would get herself some pie. That was what she would do. Pie. Lots and lots of pie. And maybe some of the gingerbread, too, unless Miles had already demolished the lot. Then she would wash it all down with hot, buttered milk. By the time she ate her way through all that, she would be too full to do anything but sleep. Either that, or she would have enough of a stomach ache to distract her from less pressing worries.

It might not be a brilliant plan, but at least it was a plan.

Amy thrust her feet into her slippers and flung a dressing gown over her night rail. She wasn't quite sure where the kitchens were, but it was no matter. A kitchen was a kitchen. How hard could it be to find? After tracking down secret agents and hidden dispatches, a large, stationary object like a kitchen should be no challenge at all.

Amy marched boldly out into the hallway and immediately pressed back into the safety of her own doorway as she heard the creak of another door being opened. A nightcap poked its head out of one of the bedroom doors, looked to right and left, and then dashed across the hallway. A brief knock and another door opened. Amy heard a muted giggle as a pale hand reached out and the man was abruptly whisked around the doorframe.

Hmm. Amy looked back and forth from one door to the other. Clearly someone was having an interesting evening.

She started forward, but the slow whine of another doorknob in motion sent her scurrying back for safety. Goodness, was everyone in Selwick Hall out and about tonight? At that rate, why not just light all the candles and call it Christmas Day already? After a few cautious moments, a door halfway down the corridor opened. Out stalked a tall, spare woman in the most alarming confection of a nightcap Amy had ever seen, bristling with bows and lace in a garish shade of purple.

As Amy watched in puzzlement, Miss Gwen strode the length of the hall, one hand shading her candle, back straight, bows on her nightcap flapping gaily, looking neither left nor right. Reaching a door at the very end, she put one ear to the wooden panel, gave a little nod of satisfaction, and coolly let herself in.

Stranger and stranger.

It was certainly a busy Christmas Eve at Uppington Hall. All that was missing was Father Christmas and Amy had no doubt he would be about sooner or later. With a shrug, Amy appropriated one of the candles from the hall table and resumed her aborted journey.

This time, she didn't even have the warning of a whining doorknob; whoever occupied this room must have brought their own oil. Instead, Amy gave a start as she found herself face to face with yet another pale-gowned figure.

"Jane!" she gasped.

Jane held a warning finger to her lips. Her pristine white nightcap perched on top of her smooth brown hair, which had been braided into a single long tail that fell nearly to her waist. She gave a quick look around. "So you figured it out, too."

Figured what out? Other than the way to the kitchen, that was. Not wanting to admit ignorance, Amy gave a quick, decisive nod.

"She just left her room," said Jane, in a hurried whisper. "If we move quickly, we can catch them before we miss too much."

Miss what? Amy wondered, nodding furiously in agreement. *Catch whom?* It was all very confusing. What had Lady Uppington put in those pies? Had everyone run mad except her?

"Come along," said Jane. "There's no time to be lost. Miss Gwen is searching her room as we speak."

"Whose room?" Amy blurted out.

Jane looked sharply at her. "Lady Jerard."

"Of course," muttered Amy. "I knew that."

Fortunately, Jane was in too much haste to enquire further. "Here. Take this." Jane extended the large object she had been holding, adding matter-of-factly, "I have my pistol."

Pistol? For Lady Jerard? What?

Automatically putting out her hand, Amy felt her wrist sag under the weight. "What is it?" she hissed, squinting in the dim light.

"A warming pan," said her cousin calmly.

"A warming—" On inspection, that did, indeed, appear to be what it was; a warming pan, with the coals removed. Amy turned it over in her hands, peering closely at the copper casing. Miss Gwen did have that sword parasol and Jane a reticule that doubled as a grenade.... "Does it turn into a crossbow, or have a sword concealed in the handle?" she asked eagerly.

"Well, no," said Jane apologetically. "But it does make a rather satisfying thunk when you clunk someone over the head with it."

Fair enough. Amy shouldered her weapon and scurried after her cousin down the length of the hallway and around a curve to a stairwell Amy hadn't been aware existed. It twisted downwards in a dizzying spiral of whitewashed walls.

Amy caught at Jane's arm as they bypassed the landing and started on a another flight. "How do you know where we're going?"

It was Amy's own ancestral-home-by-marriage and she hadn't had the foggiest idea of where half the corridors led. Other than the path between her bedroom and the main reception rooms, of course.

Jane just looked at her. Amy could see her eyebrow beginning to rise.

Not the eyebrow. She couldn't take the eyebrow just now.

"Never mind," Amy said hastily. "Forget I asked."

Silly her. Jane undoubtedly had the entire floor plan of Uppington Hall committed to memory, outbuildings and all. Just an average precaution in the day of a professional spy. That was, Amy was forced to admit, one reason why she herself hadn't lasted terribly long in the trade. She was very good at the whole dashing escapades bit, but very poor at advance planning. After all, how was one to know what one wanted to know until one was in a position to want to know it? Unless one was Jane, that was.

The winding stair spat them out onto an intricately inlaid marble floor that Amy recognized as belonging to the first floor. Jane led the way soundlessly down another corridor, pausing in front of an ornate door with a curved top, that Amy recognized as the door to the library. Richard had taken her there the other day to show her his favorite globe, the one that he had accidentally launched out the French doors and into the duck pond as a scapegrace little boy. The thought made Amy smile. But only for a moment.

How many more stories would they have time to exchange if she were to go back off to Paris?

A sharp hiss of indrawn breath brought her back to the business at hand. With a warning look, Jane held a finger to her lips and angled her head to the door.

*   *   *

Marlowe... Marvell.... Richard's finger followed an alphabetical line across the shelf of verse, but it was no use. Dead poets were all very well in their way, but their cold hands couldn't lend talent to the living.

It had really been quite poor planning on his part, his mother had opined with that irritating touch of maternal smugness, to write poetry to a teenage infatuation but not to his bride. Richard's pointing out that "teenage" and "infatuated" were the general prerequisites for the writing of poetry had left his mother unmoved.

"But Amy doesn't *want* poetry," he had argued.

"Don't be silly," his mother had said, as though he were closer to eight than twenty-eight. "All women want poetry. Especially when you've been writing it to someone else. I saw the look on her face when that dreadful Deirdre announced that she had poetry from you."

How could he explain that the look had been there already, product of homesickness for a life he had taken away from her—and then offered back to her. Somehow, the giving back hadn't worked quite as he intended. She had seemed, in fact, more upset by the cure than by the disease. Richard frowned at the elaborately embossed bindings. He knew he was missing something, but he couldn't for the life of him figure out what. With a sigh, Richard tossed Marvell and his winged chariots aside. Poetry wasn't the remedy. But since he wasn't quite sure what the remedy was, here he was, on the second floor balcony of his parents' library at three in the morning on Christmas Eve, culling the shelves for inspiration.

Merton… Milton…. *Paradise Lost* hit a bit too close to home right now. Richard picked up *Paradise Regained*, but it appeared to be entirely devoid of useful tips on how to get back to a state of grace.

Below, the library door slid inward. A female figure stepped hesitantly in. Richard glanced eagerly down, but it was the wrong woman. She was too tall, fair rather than dark. Her blonde curls glowed like a nimbus in the light of her candle. Pushing the door closed behind her, she looked from left to right, as though she were looking for something or somebody.

Blast. Deirdre. He bloody hoped she wasn't looking for him. Richard ducked behind a bust of Horace. He felt like a fool, hiding behind the statuary, but he really wasn't in the mood for another tete-a-tete, particularly not at a singularly compromising hour of the morning. With any luck, she had just come for a book to wile away the sleepless hours, and, having found one, would depart forthwith.

Funny, that. He didn't remember Deirdre being much of a reader. Of poetry or prose. But that had all been seven years ago. They had all changed in seven years. Perhaps Lord Jerard had awakened her to an appreciation of the joys of good prose. Or perhaps she was just very, very bored.

She moved purposefully towards the far end of the room. Purposeful was good. *Go on*, Richard thought, sucking in his breath and pushing as far back against the wall as he could. Horace rested on a very pointy plinth, which was doing its best to put a permanent dent in Richard's midsection. *Pick a book. Pick a book and go.*

Instead of heading for the shelves, she made for the French doors that opened out onto the snowbound garden. Richard stifled a sigh. Brilliant. That was all he needed. Soulful staring into the moon-bright night while he found himself punctured in places God had never intended.

Pushing aside one of the heavy brocaded drapes, she leaned close to the glass panel, so close that her breath left a fine fog on the glass. Holding up her candle, she moved it first to the right, then to the left, as though she were... signaling. Signaling whom?

Before Richard could speculate further, she unlatched the door with a quick, decisive motion, yanking it open with one hand. The draperies blew back as a frigid gust of air rushed into the room, and with it, the androgynous form of someone shrouded in a thick black cloak, a hood pulled low over his or her head.

"I thought I was like to freeze out there!" said in a female voice, in very colloquial French.

"English, please," said Deirdre coldly, in the sort of voice he had never heard her use before. "And keep your voice down. We don't know who else is about. The house is simply swarming with Selwicks and their brats."

Richard's jaw had relocated to somewhere in the vicinity of his waistline. What in the devil? An irreverent part of his brain speculated on exactly what his mother would have done to his former ladylove had she heard her darling grandchildren being referred to as brats. A more useful part of his brain was wondering what the devil she was about and exactly why she was conducting rendezvous with French speaking persons in his parents' library in the wee hours of the morning.

"I need more time," Deirdre was saying. "I haven't got it yet."

The cloaked figure made a gesture of displeasure. "I thought you said it would be an easy job."

Deirdre frowned. "It should have been. The wife was an unanticipated complication."

"You mean," said the other woman, with Gallic directness, "that he no longer has the infatuation for you."

"Nonsense," said Deirdre, with a smile that sent a chill right through Richard's wool coat, brocade waistcoat and assorted layers of linen. "It's simply a matter of *reminding* him."

Richard and Horace exchanged a look of masculine disgust.

"It will just take me a little more time to persuade him to confide in me, that's all. But he will," Deirdre concluded, with insulting assurance. Had he really been that much of a pushover seven years before? Apparently, yes. "For old time's sake."

Their old times hadn't been *that* good.

Below, the library door appeared to be moving of its own accord. It slid slightly and then stopped again. Their backs to it, neither Deirdre nor her companion noticed. Richard frowned down at the portal, but it appeared to have decided to stay still.

The other woman arrived at a decision. "I shall return tomorrow, then. The same time. Shall you be able to stay another night?"

Deirdre gave a nonchalant shrug. "I don't see why not."

"But I do!" This time, the door was definitely in motion. It careened open, bumping into his mother's wallhangings before rebounding back. As Richard watched, his wife charged into the room like a very short Valkyrie, waving a—was that a warming pan?—over her head like a battle axe.

His wife skidded to a halt, warming pan at the ready, and confronted the two startled conspirators. "Don't even think of trying to escape. I heard everything. The game is up!"

CHAPTER SIX

We are not daily beggars
That beg from door to door,
But we are neighbors' children
Whom you have seen before
                    --"Here We Go A-Wassailing"

Lady Jerard gave a delightful, silvery laugh. She looked with amusement at the warming pan. "What are you planning to do, heat me to death?"

Amy narrowed her eyes at her. "Burning is the usual sentence for witches."

"Dear Lady Richard." Lady Jerard moved forward with hands outstretched. "We seem to have suffered a misunderstanding."

"Indeed. You made the mistake of underestimating ME." Grasping exactly what the other woman was trying to do, Amy made a mad dash around her, intercepting the cloaked figure just before she slipped out through the French doors to safety. "Your missing maid, I presume?" she panted.

There was an undulation beneath the cloak and the tip of something dark and shiny appeared through one of the folds.

"I shall not make the same mistake," said a French-inflected voice.

Amy didn't stop to think. She swung. Jane was right; the warming pan did make an entirely satisfying thunk. She had meant to hit the pistol, but the trajectory of a warming pan wasn't quite what she had imagined it would be. She hit the maid instead. The woman went down with a thud, sending the pistol tumbling across the snagged surface of the carpet.

Abandoning her warming pan, Amy dove for the pistol. But not soon enough. As Amy skidded across the carpet, up to her elbows in rug burn, the loathsome Deirdre neatly leaned over and scooped it up. She hadn't even disarranged her hair.

"My, my," said Lady Jerard, examining the pistol as though she had never seen one before. "This does change matters, doesn't it?"

Amy really didn't like the sound of that. There was nothing like being flat on the floor on the carpet while someone pointed a pistol at one to put one at a bit of a disadvantage.

"Not really," said a voice from above. Both women twisted their heads to look up. Twenty feet up, the former Purple Gentian swung a debonair leg over the balcony railing. The rest of him looked awfully debonair, too, thought his wife fondly. All that was missing was his black cape and mask. "You, madam, are still a self-confessed traitor. And I heard it, too."

With that, he jumped from the balcony, launching himself at the broad metal ring of the chandelier.

Amy scrambled to her feet, trying to figure out if she could catch him if he fell, or if that would just mean both of them falling over and being squashed flat. For a heart-stopping moment he hung suspended from the side of the chandelier, which had gone entirely perpendicular, candles tumbling down like icicles around them. Letting go, he dropped lightly onto the balls of his feet in front of an open-mouthed Lady Jerard.

"I always wanted to do that," Richard said with a disarming grin, and plucked the pistol from Lady Jerard's hand.

Tossing the pistol to his wife, the Purple Gentian grabbed hold of Lady Jerard's arms, wrenching them behind her back in a decidedly unsentimental hold.

Amy found that she was jumping up and down like an idiot, wafting the pistol in the air and shouting things like, "Huzzah!" and "Well-played!" and "Serves you right!"

She came to an abrupt halt mid-cheer as the library door bounced open for the third time that evening. It wasn't Jane, who, having set events in motion, appeared to have made herself scarce. Instead it was... ah. Amy sobered rapidly as her mother-in-law strode into the library, looking distinctly unamused.

"What in heaven's name is going on down here?" demanded Lady Uppington, bustling into the library in a truly impressive dressing down of flowing green brocade. "It's hard enough to get the children to sleep on Christmas Eve, but at your age, one would have thought—oh."

The maternal tirade trailed to a halt as her voice caught up with her other senses. She looked from her son, holding his former beloved's arms twisted around her back, to her daughter-in-law, hopping up and down and waving a pistol in the air, to the crumpled figure lying on the floor next to a severely dented warming pan.

Lady Uppington's mouth opened and closed several times. Regaining some limited power of speech, she said, very slowly, and very carefully, "Is there something you would both like to tell me?"

Amy felt a bit as though she had been caught sticking a finger into the Christmas pudding, but Richard answered without fear.

"She is a spy," he said brusquely, giving Lady Jerard a little shake.

"Both of them," Amy contributed, gesturing with her pistol towards the huddled creature on the floor. The figure remained inert, although whether from necessity or policy remained unclear. Amy really hadn't thought she had hit her that hard.

Lady Uppington's lips set in a thin line. "Spies? Again? They're worse than moths, these spies! They get into everything. And on Christmas!"

"I don't think they've been chewing your draperies, Mother," said Richard mildly, readjusting his hold on his captive. Amy was pleased to note that it was a readjustment that placed them in less intimate proximity.

Lady Uppington looked sourly at her son. "Oh, ha, ha. But they're far harder to dispose of. One can't just swat the daughter of a neighbor. It would be too terribly awkward." She looked sternly at Lady Jerard. "Does your mother know about this, young lady?"

Somehow, through it all, Lady Jerard's clusters of curls were still perfectly arranged. She looked arrogantly at her hostess. "No."

"Hmm," said Lady Uppington. "Well, she'll have to, you know," she said, as if she were reporting some childish transgression, like jumping in the duck pond or eating all the plums out of the plum pudding. But she spoiled the illusion by adding, "And I suppose the proper authorities will have to be told. We can't have you running about doing this sort of thing again."

"Out of curiosity," said Richard, again in that mild, controlled voice, "just how long have you been doing this?"

Lady Jerard's countenance looked more than ever like porcelain, very fine porcelain, prone to cracks and jagged edges. "The first time was an accident," she said in a brittle voice. With a grim little smile, she added sweetly, "But a widow has to eke out her jointure somehow."

"Stuff and nonsense!" Lady Uppington emitted one of her infamous harrumphs. "Save the affecting tales for when you're not wearing your diamonds, my dear. If Jerard didn't leave you with a thousand pounds a year, I'll eat the Uppington emeralds."

Lady Uppington was spared making good on that culinary feat by the sound of something very large hitting the library door. It turned out to be Miles, who obviously had expected it to be locked. He barreled into the room shoulder first and kept on going. He was followed, more demurely, by a bright-eyed Henrietta, a glowering Miss Gwen, and a meek-looking Jane, all in their slippers and nightcaps.

"Is something wrong?" Jane mumbled, swaying on her feet a bit as though befuddled by sleep. She rubbed her knuckles across her eyes. "The noise woke us up."

Oooh, well done, thought Amy. If either of the spies succeeded in escaping, they would never suspect a sleepy and confused young lady, ten minutes late to the scene, of having had anything to do with their detection and apprehension.

"We all heard a racket," seconded Miles, swirling a cricket bat in the air and narrowly missing decapitating a bust of Pliny.

Assorted spies and revelations had left him unmoved, but…. "That's my cricket bat!" protested Richard.

"I couldn't find mine," said Miles, unrepentant, "and I didn't want to come down unarmed. One never knows what one might find."

"Spies," said Lady Uppington tartly, as Henrietta appropriated the bat, tucking it under her own arm for safekeeping. "Infesting the woodwork. Again."

"At least they look like small ones this time," said Miles cheerfully. "Not the big, ugly variety."

"No, just the local, treacherous variety," put in Amy.

"Spyus Neighborus," contributed Henrietta giddily. Looking at the woman standing in her brother's grasp, she added smugly, "I knew I never liked you. And it wasn't just all the awful poetry Richard was writing."

"I thought it was lovely poetry," said Lady Jerard stiffly. Amy peered closely at her. She actually appeared to mean it. Maybe she had been in love with Richard, even if just a little bit. It was an appalling thought.

Miles shook his head. "Doing it a bit too brown. Old Richard there has many talents, but verse ain't one of them."

"Oh?" said Richard. One eyebrow appeared over Lady Jerard's high-piled curls. "What about your Ode to Spring?"

"Oh, for—I was only eight!"

"Ten. 'When the leaves pop out on the tree, tra la/ And the sun shines over the sea, tra la'…."

"At least *he* had the sense to give it up before he turned twenty," Henrietta waded into the fray on her beloved's behalf.

"Sense, ha!" Miss Gwen cut off the recitation with a judicious thump of her parasol. Under the force of her glare, no one had the nerve to inquire what she was doing with a parasol inside the house, in the depths of December, at three in the morning, in the midst of a snowstorm. "If you had any sense among the lot of you, you'd think twice before leaving the library littered with the operatives of a foreign power. It is pure sloppiness."

"I suppose we shall have to put them somewhere," agreed Lady Uppington with a sigh. "And on Christmas, too. Too, too provoking."

"We could tie them up with holly and stuff their mouths with mistletoe," contributed Miles cheerfully.

"Or not," said his brother-in-law. "Can we hurry this along? My arms are getting tired."

"You could just hit her with the warming pan," suggested Amy. "I found that worked well for me. And it makes *such* a satisfying thunk."

The corners of Jane's lips twitched before she stuffed them back into their bewildered expression.

"You haven't an oubliette, have you?" demanded Miss Gwen in tones that indicated than she found the lack of one an unpardonable omission.

"Noooo...." Lady Uppington's face brightened. "The very thing! The box room. I always forget things in there. Miles, darling, if you wouldn't mind carrying the one on the floor?"

"Aye, aye." Miles smartly saluted and marched his way across the library.

"I get to search her!" sang out Henrietta, scurrying along behind.

"And I," said Lady Uppington, with a martial glint in her green eyes, "shall *personally* escort Lady Jerard. She and I have a few things to say to one another."

"Now, mother...." Richard released his hold on Lady Jerard, who haughtily shook out her skirts, looking like nothing more threatening than a society matron whose nose had been put out of joint by a mismatched seating plan or too little lobster in the lobster patties.

"Don't you 'now mother' me, young man. As for *you*, I want you to keep your hands where I can see them at all times. Try any tricks with hidden pistols and I'll have you trussed like a Christmas goose before you can say *treason*. Do we understand each other, Lady Jerard?"

Now that she was no longer being held twisted into a knot, Lady Jerard appeared to have regained some of her sangfroid. "I don't in the least understand why any of this is necessary," she said, in the soft, muted tones that accompanied her dewy-eyed look. "It's not as though I *did* anything."

"Other than waking the entire household," grumbled Miss Gwen, marching forward and taking a firm hold on the woman's right arm. "And consorting with foreign agents. Before breakfast!"

That last appeared to be the final condemnation. Consorting with foreign agents at teatime was one thing; receiving them before breakfast quite another.

"To the box room with you," said Lady Uppington firmly, taking Lady Jerard's other arm and marching her forward.

"My mother won't like this at all," retorted Lady Jerard.

Lady Uppington's voice floated back through the door. "No," she said cheerfully. "I don't imagine she will."

On that sobering note, Lady Jerard was silent.

"Up we go," said Miles, hoisting the second woman over his shoulder. A muffled squeak revealed that she wasn't quite so unconscious as she had pretended.

Amy felt a small glow of justification. She knew she hadn't hit her quite that hard.

Then they, too, were gone, Henrietta trotting along beside, issuing instructions. "Mind the doorframe! To the left—no, no, the right—mind her feet!"

"Well," said Jane brightly, as the door clanged closed behind them, blotting out the agent's anguished howl. "That made a nice little diversion. We'll have to position someone outside the box room to take down anything they might say. I imagine they'll have a good deal to say to each other once they're left alone together."

"How did you know?" Amy asked, very carefully focusing on her cousin so she wouldn't have to look at her husband. "Was it in the message you received?"

"That?" The amusement faded from Jane's face. "No. That was another matter entirely. I shan't be able to stay here long. There is trouble afoot in Paris."

"Trouble to do with royalist émigrés?" Richard asked keenly, all Purple Gentian again.

"Yes." Jane eyed him narrowly. "How did you know?"

Richard gave a debonair shrug. "Much as I would love to lay claim to omniscience... Miles told me."

"I see." Jane turned to Amy. "I need reinforcements."

This was the moment she had been hoping for, the chance to sweep back to France in a blaze of glory. And Amy realized, with a tiny flutter of panic, that she didn't want it. Not one bit.

"Really?" Amy said, trying to keep her voice as neutral as possible.

Life at Selwick Hall might not be the sort of thing that bards sang of beside the fireside when pressed for tales of heroic deeds, but there were a dozen daily amusements to keep her occupied. There was their actor-turned-butler's Role of the Week to be laughed at, the antics of their trainee spies to supervise, Richard to be argued and then reconciled with....

No, she really didn't want to go back to her brother's cold stone house in the Faubourg St. Germaine with its over-decorated reception rooms and the musty wing where her father's wigs still moldered on their stands in ever-present reminder of all she had lost thirteen years before.

"Reinforcements?" Amy echoed, her voice rusty.

Jane nodded. "I wondered if I might borrow your Miss Grey."

Miss Grey? Not her? Amy wasn't sure whether to be relieved or offended.

Relieved, she decided. Definitely relieved.

And just a little bit offended.

"*Miss Grey*? I mean, yes, of course, Miss Grey," Amy floundered. "She's done really quite well in our course."

"If you think she's ready," said Jane, with a nice degree of polite deference, "I believe I might have a role for her."

"Well, yes." Amy looked to Richard. "I think she is. Don't you?"

"Good." Jane nodded her approval as she moved towards the door. "That will be very helpful. There are too many places for me to be all at once, and others where even a disguise won't admit me. Your Miss Grey will be a vast help."

Even though she knew it was the adult equivalent of a pat on the head, Amy couldn't help feeling just a little bit pleased. It was nice to be useful, even if it wasn't the way she had initially intended. Jane was right. One person couldn't be in the same place all at once. Perhaps their spy academy might fill more of a real need than she had originally thought, rather than just being a way to pass the time.

As Amy puzzled that out, her husband took a slight, hesitant step towards her. Her stomach doing a little flip, she looked warily up at him. They were the only ones left in the room. There were too many questions hanging between them: France, Lady Jerard, France; they jammed in her throat like a half-masticated mouthful of particularly gluey Christmas pudding.

Richard cleared his throat. He was clearly having Christmas pudding problems, too.

Jane stuck her head back around the door. "Oh. I almost forgot."

Amy and Richard both looked quizzically at her.

"Happy Christmas." And the door touched back against its frame, closing Jane out, smile and all.

Well. Biting her lip, Amy turned back to her husband, who was busy examining the woodwork.

Locking his hands behind his back, he took an entirely unnecessary circular stroll, ending right back where had started. "An unusual start to the holiday."

He was being urbane again. Urbane and civil and so polished that Amy could practically see her own reflection in him. That was the thing about polish. It might be pretty, but it was fundamentally obstructive, deflecting scrutiny, masking honest emotion. If she were in a mood to be obliging, she could do the same. She could put on her best company voice and reply with the same sort of detached amusement, pretending there were nothing at all wrong with the fact that the woman whom they had apprehended had been someone he had—much as it galled her to admit it—once thought he loved. She could smile and laugh and pretend she didn't mind that there was still the prospect of separation hanging over them or that he had never bothered to come to bed that night.

It was what any good daughter-in-law of a marquess would do. Polite. Civilized. Controlled.

But she hadn't been raised to that. She might be the daughter of a viscount, but he had been a French viscount. The French did things differently. They embraced in public, kissed on both cheeks, ate the odd frog leg, and weren't afraid to admit to strong emotion. She hadn't been raised to keep a stiff upper lip and pretend she didn't feel what she felt, or to turn herself as chilly as the snow on the ground.

She would never make a proper society lady but she was what she was and that was that and if Richard hadn't figured that out when they were courting and he had caught her running about Paris in the dead of night in a pair of men's breeches, then he wasn't as bright as she thought he was.

In short, they were going to have it out now, whether he liked it or not.

Amy squared her shoulders, looked her husband full in the eye and announced belligerently, "I won't go back to France."

CHAPTER SEVEN

All out of darkness we have light,
Which made the Angels sing this night.
Glory to God and peace to men,
Now and for evermore. Amen.
                        -- Sussex Carol

Her husband shook his head. "You what?"

"You heard me." Amy folded her arms across her chest. "I'm not going, and I don't want to." That had come out the wrong way round, hadn't it? Drat. "What I mean is, I don't—"

She never got to explain what she meant. In two exuberant bounds, Richard had crossed the space between them, and she found herself squished flat against his waistcoat. "Thank goodness for that."

Amy's nose was mashed up against her husband's lapel. Not that she was complaining about the sentiment that appeared to have motivated it, but asphyxiation didn't quite constitute a full answer. In muffled tones, she said, "But you're the one who wanted me to go."

"No, I just wanted you to be able to go if you wanted to go."

Language. So confusing. There were times when Amy wondered if they might not all be better off just scratching and grunting and miming at each other, or drawing cave pictures.

"Then why did you offer?" Amy demanded, scratching her chin on the wool of Richard's jacket as she tilted her head back.

Richard eyed her warily, trying to determine whether that were a trick question. "You seemed so unhappy," he said, "about Jane."

Amy felt a little twinge of guilt. She had been. On his behalf as well as her own, she reminded herself. So, really, it had been a very generous sort of unhappiness, taking on his as well as her own. Generous, but perhaps just a little counter-productive.

"I thought you were unhappy," she countered, "about not being able to spy anymore."

Drawing himself up, Richard opened his mouth to deliver what looked like it was gearing up to be a rousing oration of denial—and closed it again.

Abandoning the pose, he deflated like a balloon, his breath whistling out beneath his teeth in a long sigh. "I was," he admitted. "I am. But not as unhappy as I would be if the situation were reversed."

"But you *were* happy there," Amy pressed. "Before."

He took a moment to think about, looking out somewhere into the space over her left shoulder, as though France might be found just to the right of the

French doors. "I enjoyed what I did," he said at long last. "A great deal. If it hadn't been for circumstances—"

"For me," Amy interjected.

"—I would probably have gone on doing it."

Amy's blue eyes narrowed. Was this supposed to be reassuring? Because if it was, he was going about it all wrong.

"*But*," Richard said, tilting back her chin to look her straight in the eye, "it couldn't have gone on forever. Sooner or later, Delaroche would have caught up with me. Even if he hadn't, one of these days, we'll finally put paid to Bonaparte's ambitions and see another king back onto the throne."

"Here, here," Amy replied by rote.

A grin flickered across Richard's lips before he sobered again. "Either way, capture or success, it had to end eventually. And where would I have been then?"

"In a French prison?" contributed Amy helpfully.

"Hopefully not. Have you seen their accommodations?"

In fact, she had, iron maiden and all. A certain member of Bonaparte's secret police had somewhat eccentric and antiquarian notions of proper interrogation methods.

"So," said Amy, summing it all up, "what you're telling me is that life with me is marginally preferable to durance vile in one of Monsieur Delaroche's deeper dungeons."

"A little more than marginally," said Richard generously. "It's right up there with one of his shallower dungeons. Ouch!" He rubbed his shoulder where Amy had whapped it. "Mid-level, then."

"And what if it had all ended in a restoration, rather than a dungeon cell?" Amy prodded.

Releasing her, Richard prowled across the carpet, kicking the warming pan out of his way. "That would have been even worse. At least in the dungeon, I could entertain myself plotting my escape and making mocking noises at my gaolers. At home...." He shrugged helplessly. "What was there to do? I've never been one for estate management. I don't find any thrill in betting large sums on the rattle of a pair of dice, and I've never been able to see the point in driving my horses too fast. Unless someone is chasing me, that is."

Amy thought about it. It was true; after their nine months together, she couldn't imagine Richard being happy with the polite dissipations that contented his peers. They were driven by boredom; Richard by something else entirely.

It was a something else that Amy understood very well, not a mere search for diversions to beguile the days, but a quest for something bigger, grander. A cause. A quest. Honor. Glory. Something with a purpose to it. Danger for danger's sake, risk for risk's sake was not enough.

Sensing he had her, Richard pressed his advantage home, "Without you," he said fulsomely, "I wouldn't have known what to do with myself. I would never have thought of starting a school for spies. I would be all alone with nothing to beguile the evenings but a pile of old newspaper clippings."

Amy snorted. "Nonsense," she said, in unconscious imitation of Miss Gwen. "I'm sure you would have found multiple candidates to share your hearth and your newspaper clippings with you."

"But they wouldn't have been you." Memory curved a smile across Richard's face. "How many women can infiltrate the dungeons of the Ministry of Police and banter with the guards in the local dialect?"

Now that he mentioned it, that had been a rather nice piece of work on her part. Even constructed on short notice, the serving wench costume had worked perfectly. Amy nodded. "True," she agreed.

Richard shoved his hands into his pockets. "I wouldn't want to go back, or change anything that happened. It's just…. " He frowned at the woodwork, scrounging for the proper words, "It is always easier to wax nostalgic about what we can't have than appreciate what we do."

It was hard to argue with that. Amy heaved a sigh deep enough to make the draperies flutter. "I've been guilty of that, too."

"About that," said Richard. "When you said you don't want to go back France… does that mean you don't want to go back?"

"I wouldn't quite put it that way," Amy hedged, even though she was the one who had in the first place. But if Richard was going to scrub his soul clean, then it was only fair that she do the same. "It's not that I don't want to go back at all. Under the proper circumstances, of course I want to go back. It all went by too fast."

Across the room, Richard shifted his weight, jamming his hands deeper into his pockets.

Taking a deep breath, Amy said definitively, knowing that she was closing a door, even as she propping open another, "But these aren't those circumstances. I don't want to go back without you."

Richard smirked. It was just a little smirk, but easily identifiable to the experienced wifely eye.

Just in case he got too smug, Amy added frankly, "In any event, I wouldn't like playing second fiddle to Jane." It was true. It had been one thing when she and Jane had been neophytes together, both learning their way in the murky world of Bonaparte's Paris. Back then, she had been the one to take the lead. To go back now, now that Jane had had eight months to build up her own methods and networks, would be impossibly galling. "I'm not very good at following orders. I prefer to be right up front, not following along behind."

Richard raised an eyebrow. "What about side by side?"

"Side by side?" Amy echoed.

Richard strolled towards her, never breaking his gaze. "Side by side," he confirmed. "A partnership. No leading, no following. I'd say we've done fairly well at that so far. Tonight, for example."

Could it really be counted as side by side when he had been up on a balcony?

Amy momentarily ignored that academic wrinkle and went straight for the more important point. "Partnership or not, we're still on this side of the Channel," she pointed out.

"Someone pointed out to me tonight that there's work to be done here, too," said Richard, and even though he kept his voice level, Amy could sense the excitement behind it. "The émigré community here is a hotbed of rumors and sedition. I know many of them from my work abroad...."

"And I don't know any of them," put in Amy, caught by the possibility. She looked up at her husband with eyes gone starry. Costumes! She would have the chance to wear costumes again and creep out back alleys and climb through windows. "You could approach them directly, while I could conduct surveillance to make sure they weren't lying to you!"

"You can reprise your serving maid performance," second her husband, enjoying himself hugely.

"And a few others," muttered Amy. "There were so many disguises I never had the chance to use...."

"If that doesn't work out," said her husband thoughtfully, "there are other countries, too. Places where no one ever saw the Purple Gentian. We couldn't go as ourselves—our names are known—but our faces aren't. We could travel safely under an assumed persona."

"Italy!" Amy's face lit up. "They've suffered under Bonaparte's yoke long enough. Or Russia. Surely, there must be work to be done there."

"The weather is better in Italy," decreed Richard. "Not to mention the food."

"We never really did have a proper honeymoon," said Amy, clapping her hands. "Where better than Italy?"

"Let's try the London route first," said her husband prudently. "Just to get back into practice first."

Amy started to argue, and then remembered that she didn't speak any Italian. Years of practicing French dialect wasn't likely to be much help in Tuscany. Perhaps a few language classes were in order before going abroad again. "Yes," she agreed demurely. "And we really can't just abandon our responsibilities at the spy school. If we go the London route, we do both at once, teaching *and* spying."

A thoughtful expression spread across Richard's face. "It could work," he said slowly. "It could work very well."

"You would have to come up with a new name, of course…"

"We," Richard corrected. "We would have to come up with a new name."

Amy abruptly ceased to envy Jane her lonely Carnation. Jane might have the notoriety, but she was a flower alone, a single bud on a bare stem, or something of that nature. Miss Gwen could only be counted as a thorn.

A husband-and-wife flower—what would the illustrated papers have to say to that? Who had ever heard of such a thing? They would take the front pages by storm. And Bonaparte, too, of course.

Amy could just picture it.

Amy beamed up at her husband. "How did you know exactly what I wanted for Christmas?" She eyed Lady Uppington's decorations. "We could be the Holly and the Ivy!"

Richard grimaced in an exaggerated fashion. "Must we?" There was a dangerous glint to his green eyes. "I much prefer mistletoe."

Amy craned her neck. "I don't see any."

"You're just not looking hard enough," said her husband blandly.

"Oh, no," insisted Amy, "I really don't think we put any in here. I should know. I hung most of it." Her hands still bore the scratches to prove it. Mistletoe wasn't quite as friendly as it pretended to be, especially when one was up on a ladder with one's mother by marriage calling out instructions.

Richard stepped closer, blotting out her view of the rest of the room. "Really?" he said, his breath ruffling the hair at her temples.

"Oh," said Amy breathlessly. "*That* mistletoe."

There would be plenty of time to work out the details of their new venture. After Twelfth Night, perhaps. As for now, her husband's former infatuation had been moved safely out of his heart and into the box room, a rosy new dawn was streaking the snow, her relatives by marriage were all safely on the other side of a very thick oak panel, and the imaginary mistletoe was calling. Amy gave herself happily up to the joy of unwrapping her very favorite Christmas present.

'Twas the season, after all.

EPILOGUE

Sussex, 2003

The train ride home always feels colder and longer than the train ride there—wherever the there may be. It wasn't quite eight by the time I made it back from Uppington Hall, but it felt much later.

I was chilled to the bone from the long ride in the unheated train and an even longer wait on the even colder platform. I had left Uppington Hall at four-thirty. That light dusting of snow had wreaked havoc on the train schedule. Admittedly, it doesn't take much to wreak havoc on the British train system. A fallen leaf, a dropped Mars bar wrapper, and, whoosh, there goes the train timetable.

The dingy white townhouses that fronted Craven Hill Gardens looked even dingier than usual in the watery light of the streetlamps as I trudged home from Paddington Station. Bulbous black garbage bags clustered around the base of the dumpsters in the center of the square, their plastic surface shimmering greasily in the lamplight. It was a far cry from marble halls and clusters of mistletoe.

Confronting the reality of modern existence, the world of two hundred years ago, the world preserved in Uppington Hall's Christmas re-enactment, seemed like Clara's dream in *The Nutcracker*, an impossible fantasy.

Despite the promises of the woman at the desk, the re-enactors hadn't been much help in finding out more about the Uppingtons in whom I was interested. They had learned their script from a later period. They were able to discourse fluently about the Selwicks who had been in their teens and twenties in 1820, Lord Peregrine, Lady Caroline, and Lord Theo. There had been portraits of the three of them—Lady Caroline with blond hair and a very firm jaw, her expression rather reminiscent of that of her Grandmother Uppington, Lord Peregrine a sturdy young man with dark hair and shrewd eyes, and Lord Theo in artistic dishevelment, doing a determined Lord Byron imitation—but I had been more interested in an earlier painting, showing the older two as round cheeked cherubs, beaming beatifically down at a plump baby kicking his legs in a basket set between them.

One of the re-enactors, the only fulltime employee of the lot, had recalled something about an embarrassing incident during one Uppington Christmas gathering, where a neighbor's daughter had been caught in a compromising situation involving French spies.

"There was a spy in the family, you know," she said seriously. "Rather famous in his day. The Purple Gentian."

When I expressed interest, she directed me to a display case in the hall, where history's flotsam had been preserved under glass. Next to a slightly bent quizzing glass and a very badly embroidered handkerchief was a page from the *Kentish Crier* of January, 1804, open to what looked to be the local gossip column, judging from all the arch references to people identified only by their initials.

A certain Lady J——, it appeared, had abused the hospitality of a local Family of Distinction by consorting with Agents of a Foreign Power. Was it due to Disappointment in Love? Did she seek Revenge for the recent marriage of a certain Former Admirer? The *Kentish Crier* left it to the reader to decide. There was a decidedly crumpled look to the page, as though someone had balled it up and thrown it across the room.

I had a very good idea who Lady J—— might be. I wasn't quite so sure as to whom had done the crumpling and throwing. It might have been any number of volatile characters. I suspected that Amy had quite a good throwing arm. So had Lady Uppington, at that.

I would have to see if I could find microfilm copies at the British Library. With any luck, there might even have been a follow-up article. But that would have to wait until after vacation. My plane theoretically left at three in the afternoon. I hoped it would. I'd been stranded in Terminal Four before.

Blowing my nose on a crumpled tissue, I shouldered my way through the front door of the narrow, white building that housed my flat. The radiator was making its usual friendly burping noises, heat and wet combining to create a smell like old mold.

Wiping my feet on the dirty, dark blue carpet, I leafed through the mail that had been left on the radiator in the hall. There wasn't much for me that day, just the annual holiday card from the head mistress of my old school and a catalogue of books from Chicago University Press. Most of my friends hadn't managed to figure out my English address, but the purveyors of catalogues seemed to have no such difficulty.

The light had burned out in the stairwell again. Either these were the shortest burning bulbs in human history, or someone was pinching them for personal use. I suspected the latter, but there was no way to prove it.

Clutching the railing with one hand, the catalogue crinkling under my arm, I picked my way downstairs in the darkness. If I were lucky, maybe *Frasier* would be on. Or *Law and Order*. There's nothing like living in another country to make you suddenly appreciate American television. My stomach rumbled hollowly beneath my coat, reminding me that Cadbury fruit and nut bar does not a dinner make. Hitching the catalogue higher up under my arm, I fumbled in my bag for my keys and tried to remember if I had any Sainsbury frozen dinners left.

Someone had gone to the take away. There was a lovely curry smell in the air that made my stomach growl in angry reproach. Perhaps I should have stopped for something on the way home. At the time, I had been so intent on getting my frozen limbs inside that it hadn't even occurred to me to think of other creature comforts. Now that I had begun to defrost, my body had time to remember other things, like food. I grimaced. There had to be a can of soup in my pantry, at least. Maybe some cereal?

Before I could get my key in the lock, the door opened of its own accord. I followed its momentum inwards, doing a very undignified stumble as someone grabbed my shoulders to keep me from going flying.

Burglars?

No. Boyfriend.

"What are you doing here?" I gasped, like any good Gothic heroine, blinking in the bright light of my foyer. Wincing, I touched my tongue to the top of my palate. I hat bitten it when I fell. Hard. I scowled at Colin. "Shouldn't you be in Sussex?"

"I decided I would rather be here?" he said. I must have looked pretty fearsome, red-nosed, teary-eyed and scowling. Not exactly a picture to cherish in one's heart during one's days apart. He added, in the tone of one dangling some nice red meat in front of an angry lion, "I brought us some take away."

Stepping back, he made room for me to squeeze past, out of the tiny corridor that doubled as both foyer and kitchenette and into my main living space, a rectangle of a room with a small round table, two twin beds pushed together to make a double, a wobbly desk, and very little else. A travel alarm clock balanced on the suitcase that doubled as a night table.

He had set out two plates on the scarred plastic tablecloth, two sets of cutlery, two wine glasses. A bottle of Greek red was open and "breathing", and the take out containers stood open in the center of the table. The curry had obviously cooled sometime ago, but I could feel the cockles of my heart warming, like an English muffin in the toaster oven.

"You didn't have to wait for me," I said, going all gooey. "You should have eaten."

Wow. A surprise return to my side; wine; and untouched food. He was clearly going for a Boyfriend of the Year award.

"I didn't think you would be that long," said Colin practically. Fair enough. As I shrugged out of my coat and scarf—fortunately, it was the scarf he had given me—he asked, "Is the BL open that late?"

"I wasn't at the BL. I went to… a museum." Call me silly, but I was reluctant to admit to having tracked his decedents to Uppington Hall. "It took me a while to get home. The Tube was acting up again."

Fortunately, Colin was concerned with more important matters. He prodded the chicken tikka masala with the points of a fork. "It may need a little…."

"Microwave," I said definitively, sweeping the container out from under his fork and bustling it off to the foyer/kitchen.

Colin followed along behind, plonking the second container down on the counter. While I rummaged for microwave safe bowls to dump the food into for heating, he roamed back into the bedroom. The remote control clicked and a voice announced more snowfall in the north before it was abruptly replaced by another voice, speaking in hushed and reverent tones about a snooker shot. Oh dear, not the snooker. Fortunately, the channel flipped again. The strident voice of Bart Simpson could be heard in the next room.

Upending the first carton and scraping the sides with a spoon, I reflected on how amazingly stereotypical it all was, me fidgeting with the microwave, Colin playing with the television. Funny, how quickly you can go from those breathless early stages of dating to placid domesticity.

I grinned to myself as I stowed the first bowl in the microwave and set the machine in motion. Well, maybe not quite that placid.

"What made you decide to skip the Sussex thingy?" I called from the kitchen as our chicken tikka spat and sizzled.

Colin wandered into the doorway, one eye on the revolving plate that held his dinner. "I wanted to spend the time with you."

This admirable sentiment was marred by the unrepentant shriek of the microwave, which cared not for such petty human affairs.

"How sweet," I said, carefully transferring the bowl to the counter and shoving the other one into the microwave in its place. Too sweet. Colin was a wonderful human being, but he was also human. And male. Sweet generally wasn't in his line. I programmed the microwave for two minutes and jabbed the start button. As the round dish began its methodical revolution, I leaned back against the counter and eyed my boyfriend suspiciously. "What's really up?"

Colin clasped his arms behind his back, the picture of wounded innocence. "Isn't wanting to see you enough?"

It was a decidedly lukewarm attempt. He knew the game was up. So did I. "No," I said firmly.

"Mmm," said Colin, looking off to the side. I could almost see the little thought bubble over his head, like one of those old Peanuts cartoons. He was thinking, *If I kiss her now, can I distract her enough that she'll forget the question, or will that interfere with the preparation of my dinner?* In a determinedly casual tone, he said, "I have to go away for a bit."

"To Italy, yes?" He had already told me that he was going to be spending the week between Christmas and New Year's with his mother and stepfather in Italy. I gathered that this was in the nature of an olive branch to his mother, but that was pure reading between the lines on my part. Colin didn't like to talk about his family. Not the live ones, at any rate. He had become slightly more forthcoming about the long dead ones, which was quite useful when I was in grad student mode, but less useful in girlfriend mode.

We had already discussed the Italy trip. It made calling schedules slightly more complicated, but it really wasn't much worse than calling England. It simply meant working around his family members.

Colin developed an intense fascination with the rotation of the microwave. "Not just Italy."

The microwave let out a long squawk but I let it go. "What do you mean?"

"I'm going to be away for a bit longer than I thought. Just some… business matters. Do you think the saag is done?" he asked hopefully, reaching for the microwave door.

I made a belated move to intercept him. "How long?"

"Not too long," he said vaguely, neatly evading me and carrying the steaming bowl to the table. "Just a few weeks."

"A few *weeks*?"

Wonderful, scented steam was wafting up from the lamb saag. My traitor stomach rumbled.

Colin poised a spoon above the bowl. "Lamb saag or chicken tikka?" he asked.

He was cunning, that one. I couldn't deny it. "Both. How many weeks? Where are you going?"

"I'll be back by the end of January," Colin said cheerfully, ladling a whopping portion of chicken tikka masala onto my plate. "Naan?"

The loud crinkling of the foil in which it had been wrapped effectively forestalled further questions.

I gave him a narrow-eyed look, a look that said, *I know what you're up to.*

Colin smiled blandly back. "Onion or garlic?"

"Onion," I said, with a sigh. "No, garlic. Oh, whatever."

He tidily tore off a half portion of each and gave me both. I looked gloomily at the little pile of food on my plate. Beware what you wish for…. Perfect boy, perfect food, and I was a perfect idiot. I couldn't decide whether I would be an idiot to interrogate him further (I could just see the Cosmo headline, "Don't

Crowd Him!") or an idiot not to interrogate him. Either way, I was an idiot.

Piling saag on his own plate, Colin cannily seized advantage of my momentary silence to change the subject. "Which museum did you go to today?"

Fine, so maybe he wasn't the only one with a secret or two. "How much naan would you like?" I asked.

He gave me a narrow-eyed look.

I crinkled the foil.

"Are you trying to make a point?" he asked darkly.

I blithely seized the opportunity and ran with it. I raised both eyebrows over the silver expanse of foil. "What point do you think I'm making?"

"Mmph," said Colin.

There's nothing like a guilty conscience to do your work for you. The only question was, what was he feeling guilty about? And where exactly was he going? Any why didn't he want me to do?

Okay, so that was more than one question. But they were all part of the same family of questions: what didn't my boyfriend want me to know?

Colin reached for the wine bottle. By tacit agreement, neither of us said anything as he filled the glasses, each weighing our options and deciding to let it go. It wasn't so much a truce as a cease fire, a temporary halting of offensives in honor of our last night together for the greater part of a month.

There were times and places for all sorts of things. Dinner, for example. And long, affectionate farewells. It seemed a shame to spoil it. Especially when it wasn't a battle it looked like I was going to be able to win. Not at the moment, at any rate.

I wondered if Amy had had this much trouble squeezing information out of her Richard. And just why their descendant was being quite so cagey if he didn't have anything interesting to hide.

It was enough to make one wonder.

"Shall we toast?" Colin suggested, lifting his glass and smiling at me. He smiled with his eyes as well as his lips. No matter what else was going on, what it was he wouldn't tell me, that smile, at least, was honest.

"Yes," I said. I lifted my wine glass in the air and looked him square in the eye. "To January."

"To January," Colin echoed. Our glasses clinked in mid-air, our eyes locked above them. My mysterious boyfriend was going to have more than a little bit of explaining to do. In January.

It was shaping up to be a very interesting New Year.

ABOUT THE AUTHOR

Lauren Willig is the author of nine novels in the bestselling Pink Carnation series, beginning with *The Secret History of Pink Carnation*, which she wrote while avoiding working on her dissertation. Subsequent Pink novels were written while avoiding law school assignments and doc review. Lauren has a BA from Yale, a graduate degree in history from Harvard, and a JD from Harvard Law. She now writes full time.